DARK LITTLE SECRETS

EVA RAE THOMAS MYSTERY - BOOK 16

WILLOW ROSE

Books by the Author

HARRY HUNTER MYSTERY SERIES

- All The Good Girls
- Run Girl Run
- No Other Way
- Never Walk Alone

MARY MILLS MYSTERY SERIES

- What Hurts the Most
- You Can Run
- You Can't Hide
- Careful Little Eyes

EVA RAE THOMAS MYSTERY SERIES

- So We Lie
- Don't Lie to me
- What you did
- Never Ever
- Say You Love me
- Let Me Go
- It's Not Over
- Not Dead yet
- To Die For
- Such A Good Girl
- Little Did She Know
- You Better Run
- Say It Isn't So
- Too Pretty To Die
- Till Death Do Us Part
- Rest In Peace
- Dark Little Secrets

EMMA FROST SERIES

- Itsy Bitsy Spider
- Miss Dolly had a Dolly
- Run, Run as Fast as You Can
- Cross Your Heart and Hope to Die
- Peek-a-Boo I See You
- Tweedledum and Tweedledee
- Easy as One, Two, Three
- There's No Place like Home
- Slenderman
- Where the Wild Roses Grow
- Waltzing Mathilda
- Drip Drop Dead
- Black Frost

JACK RYDER SERIES

- Hit the Road Jack
- Slip out the Back Jack
- The House that Jack Built
- Black Jack
- Girl Next Door
- Her Final Word
- Don't Tell

REBEKKA FRANCK SERIES

- One, Two…He is Coming for You
- Three, Four…Better Lock Your Door
- Five, Six…Grab your Crucifix
- Seven, Eight…Gonna Stay up Late
- Nine, Ten…Never Sleep Again
- Eleven, Twelve…Dig and Delve
- Thirteen, Fourteen…Little Boy Unseen
- Better Not Cry
- Ten Little Girls
- It Ends Here

MYSTERY/THRILLER/HORROR NOVELS

- Sorry Can't Save You
- In One Fell Swoop
- Umbrella Man
- Blackbird Fly
- To Hell in a Handbasket
- Edwina

HORROR SHORT-STORIES

- Mommy Dearest
- The Bird
- Better watch out
- Eenie, Meenie
- Rock-a-Bye Baby
- Nibble, Nibble, Crunch
- Humpty Dumpty
- Chain Letter

PARANORMAL SUSPENSE/ROMANCE NOVELS

- In Cold Blood
- The Surge
- Girl Divided

THE VAMPIRES OF SHADOW HILLS SERIES

- Flesh and Blood
- Blood and Fire
- Fire and Beauty
- Beauty and Beasts
- Beasts and Magic
- Magic and Witchcraft
- Witchcraft and War
- War and Order
- Order and Chaos
- Chaos and Courage

THE AFTERLIFE SERIES

- Beyond
- Serenity
- Endurance
- Courageous

THE WOLFBOY CHRONICLES

- A Gypsy Song
- I am WOLF

DAUGHTERS OF THE JAGUAR

- Savage
- Broken

Prologue
ST. AUGUSTINE

Thursday night, just before midnight

Prologue

"Help—please, you have to send someone now!"

Will's voice crackled over the phone line, his usual composure shattered into a thousand sharp-edged fragments.

"Sir, I need you to calm down and tell me what's happening," the dispatcher's voice, steady and clear, cut through the static.

"Angela—my wife—she's... she's not moving. She's lying at the bottom of the stairs. I think she must have fallen. There's so much blood." The words tumbled out in a rush, each one punctuated by the ragged edge of panic.

"Is she breathing?"

"Can't... I don't think so. I don't know. God, please. I can... I can feel a pulse. I think she's still alive, but I...."

"An ambulance is on the way. What's your address?"

"16... 164 Hawthorne Road. Hurry!"

"Stay with me, sir. Help is coming."

"Please, faster!" Will's plea was a whisper, a prayer flung into the void as he stared at his son, who was crying for his mother to wake up.

"Her eyes... they're open, but she's not.... Why isn't she looking at me?" Will's voice hitched as he knelt beside Angela, her body crumpled unnaturally. "I should be able to fix this. Fix her. I'm a doctor, damn it!" His voice rose, a crescendo of helplessness and self-reproach.

"Will, you're doing great. We're trained for this. Tell me, is there anything obstructing her airway?"

"Obstructing? No, no obstructions. Just blood. So much blood... she must have hit her head on the way down the stairs or something." His sentences were breaking, fracturing under the weight of the scene before him.

"Keep talking to me, Will. Paramedics are en route. Can you press gently on her forehead, tilt her chin up?"

His hands, which had healed so many sick children, now trembled uncontrollably as they followed the dispatcher's calm commands. He couldn't think straight. Panic rushed through him like a wildfire. "It's done."

"Good. Now, place your ear close to her mouth. Do you feel any breath?"

"I do. I do feel it. But it's so weak.... This can't be—"

"Stay with me. Check again for a pulse, carotid artery, gently on the side of her neck."

"Checking... I feel it. It's weak, though. Dear God, Angela...."

"Will, listen to my voice. Help is almost there. You're not alone."

"Please, just get them here! She needs help. I need help." His plea was raw, exposed nerves laid bare.

"Help is coming, Will. Stay with me. Stay with Angela. You're doing everything right."

"Angela, please," he whispered, his polished exterior splintered by the chaos of emotion, the relentless ticking of time.

"Angela... she's so pale, the color just—gone," Will choked out, the words a jagged shard in his throat. "She won't wake up. I can't—"

"Will, help is on the way. They'll be there any minute," the voice cut through the line, steady as an anchor in stormy seas.

"Minutes? No, that's—it's not fast enough!" His voice cracked with the tension that wired his every muscle. "She doesn't have minutes!"

"Focus on your breathing, Will. In and out. Keep her safe until they arrive."

"Safe?" he spat out bitterly, one hand pressed to Angela's icy cheek. "How is this safe?"

"Your strength is what she needs right now. You're her lifeline."

"Strength?" The word felt foreign, hollow. "I'm falling apart here!"

"Will, you are her rock. Hold on. They are close."

In the distance, faint but growing steadily louder, sirens wailed—a harbinger of hope or doom, he couldn't tell. Each moment stretched into eternity, each second a lifetime as the high-pitched keen drew nearer.

"Can you hear that, Will? That's them. They're coming for Angela."

"God, let them be quick," he murmured, almost to himself, his gaze fixed on the stairwell, willing the flashing lights to appear.

"Keep talking to me. What are you seeing right now?"

"Nothing. Nothing's changed." His voice was a frayed rope, fibers snapping one by one.

"Stay with me, Will. Stay with her. It's what you do best."

The sirens grew louder, a clarion call piercing the fog

of despair. He strained his ears, the sound promising action, demanding urgency.

"Almost there, Will. Any moment now."

"Please…." His plea was simple, a singular word carrying the weight of his world. "Hurry."

"Stay strong. For Angela."

"Angela…." Her name was a prayer on his lips as the sirens reached a crescendo outside, announcing the arrival of salvation.

"Her chest… it's not moving. It stopped, " Will's voice broke over the line, fingers trembling as he pressed two fingertips to Angela's neck. The stillness under his touch was a void, screaming silence.

"Keep trying, Will. Sometimes it's faint," the dispatcher's steady voice instructed through the phone.

"Nothing," he gasped, the word searing his throat, tasting of panic. "I can't feel anything. There's no pulse!"

"Stay calm. Paramedics are entering your neighborhood now."

"Angela, please…." His plea was a whisper as he began CPR, his cries for help drowned by the crescendo of sirens outside. He pressed, breathed, then leaned closer, his breath hitching, a prayer for a sign of life.

"Will, talk to me. What can you do right now?"

"Angela, come on!" He shook her gently, a man roused from reason by fear. His heart thundered, a wild drumbeat against his ribs.

"Will, focus on my voice. You're doing great. Help is seconds away."

"Seconds? She doesn't have seconds!" Desperation clawed at his words, raw and edging into hysteria.

"Take a deep breath. They're at your door."

"Please, just—Hurry!" His voice cracked, shattered like glass under the strain. "She's… she's everything."

"Help has arrived, Will. Let them take over."

"Angela!"

His call was a lifeline thrown into the abyss as the front door burst open, the sound of boots on hardwood flooring a staccato rhythm to the symphony of urgency that had taken over his home.

Will's gaze snapped to the doorway as paramedics rushed in, a blur of navy and fluorescent yellow. Their equipment clattered, the rapid thud of their boots syncing with the hammering of his heart.

"Here! Here!" He scrambled back, hands slick with fear, making room for them to reach Angela.

"Sir, step back," one commanded, voice authoritative yet not unkind.

"Will." The dispatcher's voice was a tether now fraying. "They've got her."

He nodded, though the dispatcher couldn't see. The line clicked dead, severance complete.

"Angela," he whispered, but the paramedics were a flurry of motion over her, blocking his view. A cuff snapped around her arm, the beep of a monitor slicing through the chaos. They continued the CPR and got a pulse back.

"Prepping for transport," someone announced.

"Stay clear," another instructed as they slid a board beneath Angela's limp form.

"Is she—" Will began, but his throat closed around the words.

"Sir, we need you to step back," a paramedic told him, eyes sharp yet empathetic.

He staggered, reaching out to steady himself against the wall while his son clung to his leg. The commotion had awakened his daughter, who had come out of her room and was now crying in his arms as well. He rubbed her hair, every movement mechanical, like he knew he was doing it but couldn't feel anything. The world tilted, sharp edges and sterile smells enveloping him. He blinked rapidly, trying to anchor himself to the moment.

"Oxygen's on. Pulse is weak, but it's there," a voice cut through the fog of his shock.

"Got a pulse," he repeated to himself, clinging to those words as if they were a lifeline.

The sirens wailed, a relentless echo as more responders arrived. Officers with stern expressions and notebooks entered, glancing between Will and the medics. Whispers of "accident" and "statements" buzzed around him like flies.

"Sir, can you tell us what happened?" an officer asked, pen poised.

"Stairs," Will managed to say. "She fell. My son found her."

"Any idea how?"

"Can't… I don't know. I was sleeping. When my boy cried for help, I ran out and found her like this."

"Okay, take a breath. We'll sort it out," the officer assured him, scribbling notes.

The stretcher's wheels clicked rhythmically as they rolled Angela toward the door. Will's eyes followed, fixated, as they disappeared into the waiting ambulance, its lights painting the night in urgent strokes of red and blue.

"Sir, we'll need you to come down to the station later," the officer said, snapping Will back to the living room, which was now a crime scene.

"Of course," Will replied, voice hollow, a shell of composure forming around his shattered state.

The ambulance doors slammed shut, a dull thud against the crescendo of the sirens that now began to fade, whisking Angela away, her life hanging by a thread.

"Angela," Will murmured once more, a vow forming amidst the chaos: to unravel the mystery of the staircase, to piece together the fragments of the night, for her. But first, he drove himself and the kids to the hospital, praying and hoping for good news.

Chapter 1
COCOA BEACH, FLORIDA

Three Years Later

I snatched the mug from the counter, the bitter aroma of freshly brewed coffee cutting through the morning chaos. My FBI badge, dangling around my neck, swayed with each hurried step, a metallic pendulum keeping time with my rising pulse.

"Kids! Shoes, teeth, backpacks—let's move it!" The words spilled out in a familiar plea, echoing against the indifference of their routine sluggishness.

"Christine, I'm not calling you again!"

My voice bounced up the stairs, grappling with the silence that mocked me from her room. She had been late every day last week and missed two whole days because she couldn't get out of bed. The school year had just started, and I wasn't having it.

"That girl is driving me crazy."

In the kitchen, Matt stood sentinel at the stove, his

prosthetic leg a testament to the resilience that pulsed through our home. Eggs sizzled in the skillet, and the scent of toasted bread wove through the air, creating a semblance of normalcy amidst the bedlam. He looked up, his blue eyes meeting mine, and for a moment, the world paused—a silent acknowledgment of shared burdens and unspoken understandings.

"Hey," I said, crossing the kitchen to him.

Our lips met briefly, a quiet storm in the pre-dawn light. His determination was as clear as the Florida sky outside, etched into the lines of his face. Our police department's cyber unit had become his new battleground, his talents blooming in binary codes and encrypted threats. He was never going into the field again, but he had found something he enjoyed just as much. He was no longer in the trenches but could still be on the front lines, fighting shadows in a digital realm.

And I couldn't be more proud of him. Reinventing yourself after losing a leg wasn't an easy thing to do.

"Morning, love," he greeted, his voice a low hum that steadied my racing heart. He plated the eggs with meticulous care, which somehow made them seem like an act of defiance against the world's chaos, or at least the chaos inside our house. "They'll listen, eventually. They're good kids."

"Eventually feels like a lifetime away," I muttered, taking a sip of the scalding liquid, letting it ground me.

The clatter of a soccer ball thudded against the fence outside. Alex had been up for a while and was already lost in his own competitive reverie.

"Alex, breakfast," I yelled out the back door, more bark than bite. My gaze flicked back to Matt, who nodded toward the stairs, a silent partner in the morning's dance—still no sign of her.

"Christine!"

This time, my admonition carried the full weight of my frustration, ricocheting off the walls as I stormed toward the staircase.

"Leave her, Eva. She'll come around." Matt's voice was a soothing balm, but the worry creased around his eyes betrayed him. Our rebellious teen was testing waters far too deep, and we both knew it.

"Fine," I exhaled, the word heavy with resignation. "But if she misses one more class…."

"Then we'll handle it. Together," he assured me, reaching for my hand to squeeze it gently.

The touch was grounding, a reminder of the partnership that anchored us. He was right; we would handle it because that's what we did. We were a team, at work and at home. And together, we'd navigate whatever stormy seas lay ahead, guiding our family through uncharted waters with unwavering resolve.

The kitchen burst into life as Angel careened through the doorway, her curly red hair a wild halo around her beaming face.

"Mommy! Daddy!" she squealed, her blue eyes alight with the remnants of sleep and dreams. "I flew like a birdie in my dream!" She flapped her tiny arms, nearly toppling over in her eagerness.

"Is that so?" I chuckled, letting the warmth of her excitement temper the morning rush. "Did you soar high?"

"Super-duper high!" she affirmed with a vigorous nod, almost losing her balance again. Matt caught her mid-giggle, steadying our little dreamer with his one good leg. He exchanged a look with me—one part pride, one part relief—his smile mirrored in mine.

"Sounds amazing, Angel," I said, ruffling her hair, now dotted with pancake batter from Matt's apron.

"Olivia, you hear that? Your sister's been flying," I called out, not expecting much of a response.

At the table, Olivia sat shrouded in textbooks, her focus unbreakable. Her short hair was now long enough to be tucked behind her ears, framing a face drawn tight with concentration. Her silence spoke volumes; she was determined to make up for what she had lost.

After partying too much the year before, the college in Colorado that had given her a full ride for running track had sent her home. She hadn't passed her classes and hadn't been running like she was supposed to. Now, she was back home, going to Eastern Florida College. I had been so angry when I found out, but seeing how hard she was being on herself for it, I realized the only way to move on was to make this a life lesson.

"College isn't just about partying," I reminded her, the words scratching at my throat. Regret tinged her expression, a fleeting shadow. I still wanted to shake her, to wake her up to the opportunity slipping through her fingers. But I bit back more lectures. She'd heard them all before.

"Mom, it's fine. I'm on top of it," she muttered without looking up. Over the summer, she met someone, a girl, and they fell in love. I had yet to meet her, as she preferred to keep her to herself.

"Make sure you are," I replied, softening my voice. Her resilience was admirable, even if it came packaged in stubbornness. It was a trait she got from me, after all. She was going to be okay. I could feel it.

"Got it," Olivia said, finally meeting my gaze. A silent promise passed between us, a truce forged in mutual respect and love. She would find her way back, I told myself. She had to.

Matt squeezed my shoulder, a quiet message of support. Our family's tapestry was frayed, threads pulling in every direction, but we were still woven together, tight and strong.

But where the heck was Christine?

I stormed up the stairs and down the hallway, my FBI badge swinging against my chest. The muffled groans from behind Christine's door grated on my nerves. I rapped my knuckles against the wood, the sharp sound echoing in the silence.

"Christine! Time to get up!"

My voice was a crack of authority in the still morning. No response. I pushed open the door, sunlight streaming in to reveal her cocooned in blankets, an arm thrown over her eyes.

"You're going to be late for school again."

"Five more minutes," she groaned, her words muffled.

"Christine, this isn't a negotiation."

I crossed my arms, watching as she burrowed deeper into the bed. Her dark hair was a stark contrast against the white pillowcase, her rebellious spirit on full display even in slumber. She had dyed it black over the summer, matching her gothic style and outfits.

"Whatever," she murmured, the defiance in her tone rising like the Florida heat outside.

"Up. Now."

It was a command, not a request. But she just turned away, and I felt that familiar tug of frustration knotting in my stomach. Was it my fault? Was I too absent, too entangled in crimes and cases, leaving my own daughter adrift?

Shaking off the thought, I left her room with a final, stern look and headed for the backyard. Through the kitchen window, I spotted Alex. His sandy blond hair was a golden blur as he darted around, a soccer ball at his feet. He kicked it hard against the fence, each thump a testament to his relentless drive.

"Alex!" I called out, sliding the glass door open. He didn't hear me; his focus was so intense on his next move and his next goal. "I'm not gonna say it again. Breakfast is ready!"

"Coming!" he shouted back without breaking stride, sending another kick into the ball that sent it flying high.

"Make sure you do, now!" I added with a sharper edge. We were already pressed for time, and I couldn't afford any delays today.

"Okay, okay, Mom!" Alex replied, his tone light but laced with that competitive edge that had him at the top of his soccer league.

"Good."

I watched him for a moment longer, his youthful energy a contrast to the weight on my shoulders. He scooped the ball under his arm and jogged toward the house, his dedication unwavering. If only I could bottle up some of that drive and pour it into Christine's morning coffee.

Closing the sliding door behind Alex, I caught Matt's eye. He was wiping his hands on a dish towel, his posture ramrod straight despite the prosthetic that now stood in place of his leg. His gaze locked with mine, and the silent communication between us spoke volumes.

"Christine," I started, my voice steady but the undercurrent of worry betraying my calm exterior. "She won't get up for school again."

Matt leaned against the counter, his brows knitted together. "How many days has it been?"

"Too many." My fingers traced the edge of my badge, the metal cool and unforgiving. "If she keeps this up...." The sentence trailed off, unfinished, but the implication hung heavy between us.

"She's smart, Eva," Matt said, his tone reassuring but

not dismissive. "She's just going through a phase, you know? Teenagers."

"Is it just a phase?" I countered, feeling the frustration bubble up inside me. "Or is it because I'm—"

"Stop that," he cut in, firm yet gentle. "You're an incredible mom. You can't be here every second; we both have jobs that matter. She knows that."

I sighed, the sound mingled with the hiss of the coffee machine behind me. "Jobs that matter," I echoed, the words tasting bitter. "But at what cost?"

Matt limped forward, closing the distance between us. His hand found mine, squeezing it in silent solidarity. Our partnership was more than just work; it was a lifeline in moments like this.

"Christine will graduate," he stated with conviction. "She's a fighter—like her mother."

"Sometimes, I wish she didn't have to fight so hard." My eyes found his, searching for the reassurance that I couldn't seem to muster for myself.

"Hey, we'll get through this. Together." His thumb stroked the back of my hand, grounding me.

I nodded, absorbing the strength from his touch. "Together," I repeated, allowing myself to believe it.

Chapter 2

Diane Matthews knelt in her garden, the California sun warm on her back as she tended to her roses. With practiced fingers, she snipped a wilting bloom, the scent of fresh earth and petals surrounding her. The gentle hum of bees and the distant laughter of children filled the afternoon—until the shrill ring of her phone sliced through the serenity.

"Hello?" Diane's voice was the soft caress of a breeze through the leaves.

"Diane Matthews?" The voice on the other end was gruff, edged with formality.

"Yes, this is she."

"Detective Mark Larson here, Saint Augustine Police Department." The pause that followed was heavy and loaded. "I'm afraid I have some disturbing news about your son-in-law, Will."

The pruning shears slipped from her fingers, thudding against the soil. "Will? What's happened?"

"Ma'am, he's been arrested for the murder of your daughter, Angela."

"Murder?"

The word was a foreign invader in her mouth, bitter and jagged. "But... but I don't understand. It was an accident. She got up in the middle of the night and fell down the stairs. She died in the ambulance. That's what we were told. They—you—said it was an accident. This can't be true. It must be a mistake."

"I understand this is hard to accept," the detective continued. "Especially after so many years."

"Hard to accept?" Diane's voice crescendoed, a rare sharpness slicing through her usual calm. "It's more than that. It's impossible. Someone must be mistaken."

"Ma'am, the evidence brought to light—"

"Will loved Angela," she interjected, her tone insistent, unyielding. "He could never harm her. There's been some sort of error."

"Unfortunately, the arrest is based on new findings in your daughter's case. New evidence has been brought to the light of day."

"New findings?" Her heart raced, each beat a drum echoing her mounting dread. "I can't believe this. How? Where is this all coming from? I thought the case was closed years ago? I can't... you know what? I'm coming to St. Augustine. I will be there. I will get to the bottom of this."

"And you have every right to, but it won't change the facts. The case has been reopened, and Will Jennings has been arrested."

"That's nonsense. I don't believe this. We can talk when I get there. I need to know everything."

"Very well, we'll await your arrival. Thank you, Mrs. Matthews."

"Thank you?"

The words hung empty in the air as the line went dead.

She stared at the phone, disbelief etched into every line of her face—the garden around her blurred, her sanctuary now a prison of unanswered questions and rising fear.

Will arrested? For murdering Angela? After three years? It can't be right.

Diane's hands, once steady and sure among the petals and leaves, now trembled as she dialed the traveling company she usually used.

"I need the next flight to Florida," her voice was steel wrapped in velvet, a testament to resolve born from a mother's fierce love.

"St. Augustine," she added, urgency knotting her words into terse commands.

"Please hold for available flights," the agent replied, a distant voice against the storm brewing inside her.

She paced, phone pressed to her ear, each step a silent vow to clear Will's name, to right this inconceivable wrong. The garden outside faded to a mere backdrop; her mind raced ahead to Florida, to courtrooms and confrontations.

"Your confirmation number is," the agent's voice returned, slicing through the cacophony of her thoughts.

"Thank you," Diane hung up, not a second lost, not a single breath wasted on pleasantries.

Her suitcase lay open, a cavernous maw ready to swallow the essentials for battle. She folded clothing with precision, an armor against the days ahead. Her fingers skimmed over Angela's photo before tucking it safely between layers of fabric—a talisman against doubt.

"Justice," she whispered to the image, a promise etched in her eyes, still sparkling with undiminished determination.

The taxi honked outside the next morning, a clarion call to action. She hefted her luggage, every ounce of its weight a testament to what she carried inside: conviction, unwavering belief, and a mother's indomitable spirit.

"To the airport, please," her directive cut through the early morning haze, the cityscape blurring past, a tableau of lives untouched by her turmoil.

Diane Matthews was en route, a force of nature set upon a course that brooked no interference, no delay. Her son-in-law's innocence was the beacon guiding her, and her daughter's memory was the fuel igniting her onward.

Chapter 3

Diane stepped off the plane in Florida, the humid air enveloping her like an unwelcome embrace. St. Augustine greeted her not with open arms but with an inscrutable face. She navigated through the airport, her senses tuned to every detail—the scent of sea salt mingling with jet fuel and the lazy spin of ceiling fans that fought a losing battle against the heat.

She found herself outside, the rental car kiosk a beacon amidst the chaos. Diane approached, her stride confident, her request for a vehicle straightforward. There was no time for hesitation, no room for second-guessing.

"Something reliable," she stated, locking eyes with the employee, whose fingers danced across the keyboard, securing her request.

"Will this work?" he asked, sliding the keys across the counter.

"Perfectly," Diane said, snatching them up. The keychain felt solid, a small piece of control in her grip.

The drive to the Airbnb was a blur—a stream of traffic

lights and palm trees that lined the streets like sentinels. She pulled up to the address, the house modest, its facade bathed in the golden hue of the setting sun. Palmettos rustled in the gentle breeze, whispering secrets of the town they guarded.

Diane killed the engine, and silence flooded the car like water. For a moment, she allowed herself to breathe, to feel the full weight of her presence in this foreign place.

She grabbed her suitcase and stepped out. With each step toward the front door, Diane Matthews reaffirmed her purpose—she was here to exonerate Will, to honor Angela's memory.

And nothing would stand in her way.

The lock clicked open, and Diane stepped into the Airbnb, her heels tapping against the tiled floor—a crisp staccato in the stillness of the room. She scanned the space: an open-plan living area kissed by the fading light, sparse furniture dotted around, promising comfort without sentimentality. It was exactly what she needed.

She unzipped her suitcase, methodically transferring clothes into the dresser. Each garment had a crisp fold, and each placement was precise. Her hands moved with practiced efficiency; this was not the time to dwell on the softness of the fabric or the memories stitched into it.

Settled in, Diane perched on the edge of the cream-colored couch, closing her eyes briefly. A deep breath in and out, and then she was up again, determination flooding her veins like adrenaline.

. . .

DETECTIVE LARSON'S office was clinical, all sharp angles and sterile smells. Diane's eyes met his, unwavering, as she took the seat across from him without waiting for an invitation.

"Detective," she began, her voice a tempered blade. "I want to understand why you've arrested my son-in-law."

"Mrs. Matthews," he said, leaning back. "It's procedure to—"

"Procedure doesn't arrest an innocent man." Diane cut him off. "Angela's death was an accident; that's what I was told. Now you're saying Will is responsible?"

"New evidence has come to light," Larson replied, his gaze steady but not as sure.

"Then share it," Diane insisted, leaning forward. "I need to see it for myself."

"Mrs. Matthews, it's not that simple—"

"Make it simple," she snapped, the nurturing facade momentarily slipping. "My family has suffered enough. I won't let you railroad an innocent man because you need a quick close to the case. He is the father of my grandchildren."

Larson's eyes narrowed slightly, and then he shook his head. "I'm sorry. But it's confidential."

"Well, I guess I'll have to get it another way," Diane said, her composure returning. "I assure you, Detective, I will find the truth. And when I do, I expect your full cooperation."

"Mrs. Matthews, there is no other way to…."

"Where there is a will, there is a way. And I always find my ways," she said with a slight hiss as she stood.

He didn't respond, watching her instead with a mix of respect and wariness. Diane met his silence with a curt nod.

"Good day, Detective Larson. I trust we'll be speaking again soon."

With those final words, she turned on her heel and strode from the office, the door swinging shut behind her with a decisive click.

THE CLANK of metal doors reverberated as Diane Matthews stepped into the sterile visiting room, her heart thrumming against her ribcage. She spotted Will through the glass partition, a shadow of the man she remembered. Their eyes met, a silent exchange of sorrow and resolve.

"Will," she said, pressing the phone to her ear, her voice steadying at the sight of him. His hand lifted to the glass, a gesture that bridged the distance between them.

"Diane… thank you for coming." His voice was a hoarse whisper.

"Nothing could've kept me away," she replied, clutching the receiver like a lifeline. "We're going to get through this. I'm here to help." I will get you the best lawyer money can buy around here. I will get you out so you can be with your children again."

"Angela would be grateful," he said, his eyes glistening with unshed tears.

"Angela knew my love has no bounds," Diane affirmed, her words a fierce whisper. "And I know you're innocent."

They talked of memories and hope until the guard's stern voice announced that time was up. Diane stood, her hand lingering on the cool glass.

"I'll be back soon," she promised before the door buzzed and swallowed her back into the world.

. . .

THE LAWYER'S office was a stark, utilitarian space, all sharp angles and cold light. Diane sat across from Mr. Stevenson, his suit immaculate, his gaze calculating.

"Mrs. Matthews, I won't sugarcoat it. This is an uphill battle," Stevenson began, shuffling papers with precision.

"Then we climb," Diane cut in, her tone edged with steel. "Tell me the plan."

He outlined motions, appeals, and expert testimonies. She cataloged each word and strategy with a methodical focus.

"Forensics will be key," Stevenson said, tapping a finger on a stack of reports. "If we can discredit the evidence—"

"Discredit?" Diane interjected. "Or prove it wrong? There's a difference."

"Proving it wrong will be difficult," he admitted, locking eyes with her. "There's a new witness; that's all I've been told. We can, however, discredit other aspects of the investigation, maybe even find faults, and perhaps get the whole trial declared invalid, a mistrial. That would be my approach."

"Difficult doesn't mean impossible," she retorted, leaning forward. "We must keep him out of jail at all costs."

Stevenson nodded, but his skepticism was tangible, hanging heavy in the air. Diane bit back frustration, her mind racing. Every second mattered, every detail a potential key to unlocking Will's cell.

"Leave no stone unturned," she stated, more a command than a request. "I'll be doing the same."

"Understood," Stevenson conceded, though his expression remained unreadable.

Diane rose, her movements crisp and purposeful. She had planted seeds of hope; now, she needed them to take root. The fight had just begun.

Chapter 4

I had barely nudged the front door closed when Christine's final, frantic steps faded into the morning bustle, and she left for school. A sigh of relief escaped me—all kids had been dispatched, and another day had begun. Matt's arms found their way around me, and we shared a quick, comforting embrace.

"We need to get better at this," we muttered in unison, laughter softening the edges of our morning chaos.

"More coffee?" Matt asked, his voice the audio equivalent of a warm blanket.

"Yes, please. I have time for one quick one."

The aroma of freshly brewed coffee seemed to fill the void left by the children's departure.

We sat, mugs cradled in our hands, exchanging idle chatter about nothing and everything when the shrill ring of my phone sliced through the calm.

"That didn't last long," I quipped, thumbing the answer button.

"Eva Rae Thomas?" The voice on the other end was

tinged with an urgency that put me on alert. "Agent Eva Rae Thomas?"

"Speaking."

"Hi, Eva Rae… It's Diane Matthews. I know your mother."

Recognition sparked immediately. Diane Matthews was a good friend of my mother's and had been for all the time I could remember. I could almost see her—poise, elegance, always a kind word. I had known her since I was a child but hadn't seen her in many years.

"Of course, Diane. How can I help you?"

Her breath hitched over the line, words rushing out like floodwaters breaching a dam.

"Something terrible has happened."

I set my coffee down, my grip tightening on the phone as she spoke. The lightness of the morning began to dissipate, shadowed by Diane's despair. I remembered my mother telling me what happened to Angela, her daughter, who died in a tragic accident. What could possibly be happening now?

"Tell me what's going on, Diane."

"Angela's husband, Will… they've arrested him for murder. They think he killed Angela, but he didn't do it, Eva Rae. He couldn't have. It's all such a terrible mess."

Murder. The word hung heavy, a dark cloud threatening a storm. I leaned forward, elbows on the table, every fiber of my being attuned to her plea.

"Please, Eva Rae. You're the only one I can turn to. I need your help."

I listened while my mind raced, piecing together the fragments of a picture I hadn't yet seen. Her voice quavered, each word weighted with fear and the raw edge of desperation.

The gravity of the situation settled over me like an

unwelcome cloak, the familiar tug of duty pulling at my conscience. This was more than a cry for help; it was a call to arms.

"Could you please come to St. Augustine?" she asked.

St. Augustine? The words snagged in my mind; it was far from home, from the kids who needed me.

"Diane, I… this isn't a good time. My family, the kids, they're just settling into their routines."

"Please, Eva Rae, I wouldn't ask if it weren't urgent." Her voice was a tightrope, quivering with tension.

I glanced at Matt, his brow furrowed, eyes locked on mine. The silent conversation we shared spoke volumes of concern and understanding—a mother's plea, a family's need. My chest tightened; the balance between duty and devotion was never steady.

"Can you tell me more about what happened?" I hedged, buying time, my heart thrumming against my ribcage.

"Will is innocent, but no one will listen. You have that intuition, Eva Rae, you have experience, you can see what others don't."

The call to justice was a siren song, seductive and demanding. But the thought of leaving, the image of Angel's face, Alex's soccer games missed—each a thread pulling taut.

"Money isn't an issue," Diane pressed, sensing my hesitation. "We'll compensate you generously for your time away from your family."

"Generously…," I echoed, the word foreign. We had been having money trouble lately. Heck, we always did with all these children. The house was a money pit on top of it all. It would help us a lot.

"Whatever it takes, Eva Rae. I'm begging you."

I swallowed hard, the weight of her desperation anchoring me to the spot.

"Give me a moment, Diane."

I muted the call, the silence stretching thin. Matt's hand found mine, a lifeline in a roiling sea.

"Think about what you need, Eva Rae. Not just the money, and not just the job. What do you need?"

His question was a beacon through fog, clarity inching forward. I was a mother, a partner, a defender of the innocent—my identity stitched from many fabrics.

"Okay," I breathed out, unmuting the call. "I'll take the case, Diane."

"Thank you, Eva Rae. Thank you."

I pocketed the phone, my decision made. But as I met Matt's gaze, doubts gnawed at me, sharp-toothed and persistent.

Was this the right thing to do?

Chapter 5

My phone clattered against the kitchen counter as I swung into motion, thoughts already racing to logistics and contingencies. I hurried up the stairs and rummaged through drawers for my travel checklist, the paper worn at the edges from use.

"Olivia, hey, it's Mom," I spoke into the phone, securing it between my shoulder and ear as I folded clothes into my duffel bag—shirts, slacks, and other essentials.

"I need a favor. I have to go away on an assignment for the next few days. Can you watch over the others while I'm… away? Matt will be here, but he will also need to work. So maybe you can help him out a little around the house?"

"Sure, Mom." Olivia's voice crackled with static, but her assurance was clear. "Is everything okay?"

"Everything is fine. Just another case," I replied curtly, not wanting to worry her with details. "I'll explain later."

"Okay, Mom. Have a good time, and be careful, okay?"

"I promise," I said and hung up.

"Matt, can you help Alex with his soccer practice this week?" I called out, crossing the room to where he worked at his desk, his fingers deftly maneuvering across his keyboard.

"Already on my schedule," Matt said without looking up, a soft smile in his voice. He knew the drill—our life was a constant shuffle of responsibilities.

I grabbed my phone again.

"Chief Annie," I began as the call connected, my voice steady despite the storm brewing within. "I've got a situation that requires me to head to St. Augustine. Is that okay?"

"Go," she replied crisply. "We've got your back here."

"Thank you," I murmured, grateful for one less hurdle. With a final zip of my duffel, my gaze swept the room, a mental inventory ticking off each item.

Matt got up and walked to me. His hand found my shoulder, grounding me.

"You've got this, Eva Rae," he reassured me. His eyes, steadfast and sure, met mine, bolstering my resolve.

"Thanks, Matt," I said. "It means more to me than you think."

"Go get 'em."

The weight of the duffel bag on my shoulder mirrored the heaviness in my chest. Potential risks flickered through my mind like a slideshow of nightmares—dead ends, danger, the unknown. I could feel the pull of uncertainty, the whisper of fear that clawed at the edges of my determination.

"Be safe," Matt said, his words a lifeline as he opened the door for me.

I nodded, my response locked behind a tight throat. The warm Florida sun greeted me. My hand hesitated on the car door, doubts circling like vultures over a carcass.

"You're not doing this for yourself but to help people in need," I whispered to myself, a mantra to quell the disquiet. "You're doing it for Diane and for Will, heck even for Angela, who wouldn't want her husband to be wrongly accused of her murder."

I slid behind the wheel, the engine coming to life with a reassuring purr. The rearview mirror captured Matt's figure retreating into the house—a snapshot of what I was leaving behind and a reminder of what I was fighting for.

With a deep breath, I shifted into drive and pulled away, the road stretching ahead, both an invitation and a challenge. Right thing or not, I had made my choice. And there was no turning back now.

Chapter 6

THEN:

Will Jennings navigated the wedding venue with practiced ease, his eyes scanning the room as he exchanged handshakes with the other guests gathered to celebrate their mutual friends' big day. They were drawn to him, his laughs punctuating the hum of conversation, his smile contagious.

"Will, good to see you!" someone exclaimed, clapping him on the shoulder.

"Wouldn't miss it," Will replied, his voice steady, an undercurrent of something deeper within.

The doors at the far end of the hall swung open, and then she entered. Angela Matthews. A vision in her understated elegance, her blonde hair catching the soft light, her blue eyes bright. Her mere presence caused heads to turn everywhere. Will's gaze lingered. She moved through the crowd, unaware yet of the gravity she wielded, her presence pulling him like a tide.

Their eyes met. It was an accidental collision of stares

across the distance. Will's smile deepened, genuine for a moment, and Angela's lips curled into a responding smile, subtle but unmistakable. The air around them seemed charged, the world narrowing to the space between their glances.

"Beautiful ceremony, wasn't it?" he said later at the reception, easing closer to where she stood by the window, her silhouette framed against the setting sun.

"Absolutely," Angela agreed, turning toward him, the light playing off her features. Her tone was soft, her words deliberate.

"Stunning view, too." He gestured outside, but his eyes stayed on her.

"Quite stunning," she echoed, her gaze not leaving his.

A laugh burst out from a group nearby, breaking the spell, and they both looked away. But the connection, once made, was not easily undone. They were aware of each other now, their awareness mingling with the laughter and the clink of glasses, adding another layer to the evening's tapestry.

Will slid into his assigned seat at the dinner, the linen napkin crisply folded before him. He glanced at the name card next to his, and a flicker of surprise danced across his features. "Angela Matthews," he read aloud just as she approached with a graceful stride.

"Looks like fate's playing matchmaker," Angela quipped, her voice light, settling into the chair beside him.

"Or it has a sense of humor," Will countered, offering her a conspiratorial grin.

"Let's hope for both," she said, returning the smile.

Their laughter mingled with the soft clinking of silverware and murmurs of other guests. As the first course arrived, an array of delicate appetizers, their conversation flowed naturally, like a stream finding its path down a hillside.

"Medicine was always my calling," Will shared, his eyes alight with a fervor that went beyond mere career choice. "There's a thrill in the challenge, in unraveling the mysteries of the human body. Especially in children. I just love taking care of children, so that's why I chose pediatrics."

"Saving lives and loving children on top of it all, " Angela mused, admiration lacing her words. "Quite the combination."

"Every patient is a story," he continued, "and there's nothing more rewarding than adding a positive chapter to it."

"Spoken like a true hero." Her tone held warmth and a touch of playfulness.

Will blushed. No one had ever called him that.

"Hardly a hero," Will demurred with a gentle shake of his head. "Just someone who tries to make a difference."

Angela leaned in, her blue eyes sparkling mischievously. "So, Dr. Jennings, you solve mysteries of the body. Ever encounter any you couldn't crack?"

"More than I'd like to admit," Will confessed, an appreciative grin tugging at his lips. "But those are the cases that teach you the most."

"Ah, a perpetual student." She nodded sagely. "Humility in a doctor—I thought that was an urban legend."

"Only as rare as an easygoing wedding guest," he shot back with a playful glint in his eye.

Their banter danced between them, light and quick-footed. Angela's laughter, bright and genuine, filled the space around them with a warmth that seemed to draw others into their circle, yet they remained ensconced in their own private world. There could have been a thousand people in the room, and they would never have noticed.

"Speaking of legends," she continued, reaching for her glass, "I heard about a curious case from a friend in pediatrics. A real medical mystery, right here in the city."

"Is that so?" Will leaned closer, intrigued. "Do tell."

As she recounted the tale, her hand gestured animatedly, fingers brushing against his momentarily—a whisper of contact that sent a jolt through him, potent and unexpected. Their eyes locked, and for a heartbeat, the surrounding chatter faded into the background.

"Seems like your kind of challenge," she concluded, her voice now softer, somehow more intimate.

"Sounds like it." His response came out just a tad huskier than intended. "Perhaps we could discuss it further over coffee sometime?"

"Maybe we should," Angela agreed, the corners of her mouth lifting in a smile that promised shared secrets and the thrill of discovery.

The evening air seemed to thicken around them, charged with anticipation. Their connection deepened with each beat of the music, each shared glance.

The string quartet surged into a crescendo, their bows dancing furiously as Will and Angela swayed to the rhythm of the waltz. The grand ballroom was bathed in the soft glow of crystal chandeliers, casting prismatic light across the walls like scattered jewels. Laughter rippled through the air.

"Ever imagined yourself in a fairy tale?" Angela's voice was a whisper over the music, her eyes alight with the reflection of golden beams.

"More of a wilderness guide than a prince," Will replied, a half-smile playing on his lips.

Their movements were fluid, two figures gliding amidst a sea of celebrants. A floral scent drifted from the centerpieces, roses and lilies vying for dominance. The rich taste of chocolate still lingered on their tongues from the decadent wedding cake that had been cut moments ago.

"Yet here you are, leading the dance." Her fingers tightened slightly on his shoulder.

"Only because I found a willing partner."

A laugh escaped her, lost in a swell of violins. His hand rested at the small of her back, a touch both protective and possessive. She followed his lead, every step an unspoken promise.

"Angela!" A voice cut through the melody. Heads turned. It was the bride, radiant in layers of lace, her eyes bright with mischief. "Catch!"

The bouquet arced through the air, a streak of green and pink. Time slowed as it spiraled toward them. Guests held their breaths. Angela reacted instinctively, reaching out to pluck it from its flight. The room erupted in cheers.

"Seems fate has a sense of humor," Angela quipped, the corners of her eyes crinkling with amusement.

"Or a flair for the dramatic."

Their eyes locked, a silent conversation taking place. The world shrank to the space between them, charged with possibility. Her hand brushed against his, a spark leaping at the contact.

"May I steal you away?" His voice was a low rumble, barely audible above the orchestra playing.

"For a breath of fresh air?" she countered.

"Something like that."

They slipped away, unnoticed by the crowd. Outside, the night was alive with the symphony of crickets and the gentle murmur of distant conversations. Moonlight painted the garden silver, shadows playing hide and seek among the bushes and statues.

"Angela," he began, his words trailing off as he turned to face her.

"Tell me," she urged, stepping closer.

"Would it be too rash—?"

His sentence was cut short as a sudden commotion erupted from the ballroom behind them—shouts and the crash of something breaking. Instinctively, they moved together, backs touching as they peered through the French doors.

Inside, the music had stopped. A figure lay sprawled on the dance floor, motionless, the crowd parting in shock. Panic began to ripple through the guests, a wave of horror washing over the celebration.

"Is that—?" Angela started, but Will was already moving.

"Stay here," he commanded, not as a request but as a necessity.

"Will!" she called after him, but he was gone, swallowed by the throng rushing to aid the fallen guest. Angela stood alone, the bouquet clutched in her hands, her heart racing. Without warning, what had begun as a night of enchantment had turned into a scene fraught with danger.

And just like that, the fairy tale was shattered.

Will surged forward, his heart pounding against his ribs. His polished shoes slipped on the glossy floor as he dodged a tangle of guests. Their faces blurred past him, expressions ranging from shock to disbelief.

"Make way!" His voice, firm and authoritative, cut through the clamor. "I'm a doctor!"

The lights overhead flickered, casting an eerie glow across the scene before steadying. Time seemed elastic, stretching and collapsing with each step he took toward the motionless figure.

"Call 911!" someone shouted behind him.

"Already did!" another voice responded, tinged with panic.

He reached the circle's edge. The fallen guest was face down. Will crouched, his fingers searching for the pulse at his neck—there was none.

"He's in cardiac arrest. Help me turn him over," he instructed, looking up at the hesitant bystanders. A pair of hands joined his, and together they gently rolled the guest onto his back.

"Clear some space!" His voice pierced the chaos, his command resonating in the suddenly hushed room. He started to perform CPR, grunting as he pressed on the man's chest. Frantically, he continued until the man came back to life.

"Someone get a cushion or a jacket!" Will's gaze didn't waver from the guest's pale face, now groaning softly, life fluttering back into alarmed eyes.

"Here!" A jacket was thrust into his hands, which he folded and placed under the man's head.

The guests receded like a tide going out, their murmurs fading. Angela remained rooted to her spot, watching Will with an intensity that spoke volumes. She could sense the danger lurking beneath the surface, the darkness that had been threatening to spill forth all evening.

"Stay with me," Will urged the guest, whose eyes fluttered open once more.

"Wha—what happened?" the guest croaked.

"We're figuring that out," Will assured him, his focus unwavering. "You're safe now."

"Safe," the man echoed weakly, a tremor in his voice.

"Paramedics are here." The groom's statement was both gentle and decisive.

"Good." Will nodded, rising to his feet. "You're going to be okay."

As medics arrived, a stretcher weaving through the thinning crowd, the once-celebratory atmosphere was now laden with concern and whispers of speculation.

"Will?" Angela approached tentatively, uncertainty etched into her features.

"Everything's under control," he told her, though his expressive eyes hinted at the storm raging inside him.

"Thank you," the guest mouthed to Will as he was carried away.

"Take care," Will replied, the gravity of the night pressing down upon him.

Angela reached out, her touch light on his arm, grounding.

"Come on," she whispered, guiding him away from the center of turmoil. "Let's find some air."

The night air engulfed their skin as they emerged from the chaos, a cathedral of silence enveloping them beneath the moonlit sky. Angela's grip on Will's arm was both delicate and determined, her presence an anchor in the tumultuous sea of the evening's events.

"Deep breaths," she coached softly, her voice cutting through the quiet with precision. "You were amazing in there. You saved that man's life. You really are a hero."

A shared silence fell between them, comfortable yet charged, their connection deepening beyond mere words. The night stretched on, witness to the subtle shift in their dynamic, a newfound intimacy blossoming under the watchful stars.

Angela looked at him, her eyes filled to the brim with

admiration. Then she rose on her tippy toes and kissed him.

Chapter 7

I pulled up to the Airbnb in St. Augustine; the sun's glow reflecting off the old Spanish architecture gave the city a kind of burnished, antique look. I could feel it—the urgency, like an electric current coursing through my veins as I grabbed my bags from the back seat and made a beeline for the front door.

"Here to visit someone?" The host, a wiry man with salt-and-pepper hair, asked as he handed me the keys.

"Nope. Here for work, not pleasure," I replied curtly, my mind racing ahead to the tasks at hand. I didn't bother with pleasantries; there wasn't time. I took the stairs two at a time, found the door to the house, and let myself in. The place was quaint, a painting of coastal serenity that I barely registered. My bags hit the floor with a thud, their contents forgotten as my phone began to vibrate in my pocket.

"Thomas," I answered without looking at the caller ID.

"Eva Rae, it's Diane Matthews." Her voice was laced with distress, tugging at my instincts.

"I just got here," I said. "Checking in as we speak."

"Good. We need to talk."

"Tell me where and when," I said, moving toward the window, already scanning the street below for any signs of trouble.

"O'Steen's on Anastasia Boulevard. Can you make it now?"

"Give me ten minutes." I ended the call and tucked the phone away, my brain firing on all cylinders.

I left the house as swiftly as I had entered it, the sense of purpose driving me forward. The air was humid against my skin as I made my way to my car. Every tick of the clock was a reminder of what was at stake—a family torn apart by tragedy and accusation.

As I started the engine, the threads of the case began to weave together in my head, forming a tapestry of questions and possibilities. What new evidence could possibly point to Will? And why now?

The drive was short, yet every red light felt like an eternity, every slow-moving car in front of me an obstacle to my mission. When I finally parked outside O'Steen's, my heart was pounding—not with fear, but with the adrenaline of a huntress on the scent of truth.

I pushed open the door to O'Steen's. The room was dimly lit, laughter and chatter underscored by the soft strumming of a guitar from the corner stage, where some guy was entertaining the guests between fish dip and conch fritters. I took it all in with a swift glance—patrons huddled over their meals, a tender moment at the bar—but my gaze sliced through the ambiance, homing in on my sole interest.

There she was, Diane Matthews, sitting at a corner table as if she owned the shadows that danced around her. Time had dared not to lay a finger on her; her dark hair cascaded with the same shine as those years ago, defying the very notion of aging. She sat there, an embodiment of grace under the dim lights, her poise untouched by the gravity of our meeting.

"Ms. Matthews," I started, approaching her with purpose. Her head tilted up, those deep blue eyes locking onto mine—a silent conversation before words could even escape.

"Eva Rae," she said, her voice a soothing melody amidst the hum of conversations. "It's been too long."

"Far too long," I agreed, the warmth in her tone thawing the usual frostiness of my demeanor. We embraced briefly, a shared history folded into that simple act.

"Sit, please." Diane gestured to the chair opposite her, her movements fluid, her elegance unwavering even in something as mundane as an invitation to sit.

"Thank you for coming on such short notice," she said, folding her hands on the table, her eyes never leaving mine.

"Of course, Diane," I replied, matching her intensity.

Diane's eyes sparkled as she leaned in, her voice a conspiratorial whisper. "I've followed your career, Eva Rae. FBI agent. Profiler on many important cases. Books written. It's impressive."

"Thank you, Diane," I managed, the praise unfamiliar yet not unwelcome. I was often too hard on myself when thinking of what I had accomplished and where I had failed.

"Your mother… she may not wear her heart on her sleeve, but she's proud. I know it."

My smile faltered, a tightness gripping my chest. A flash of memory—my mother's indifferent gaze across a dinner table, reports of my accomplishments met with a nod, nothing more. Pride? That was an alien concept in my family.

"Maybe," I said, words clipped, betraying nothing of the internal chill that the mention of my mother always stirred. She was better than she used to be, and that was at least something.

I sipped water, cool and detached as my thoughts. The contrast struck me—Diane's warmth against the frost of my own maternal bond. Support was something I learned to find elsewhere, to build from scratch like a case with no leads.

Diane's hands trembled as she clasped her sweet tea.

"Angela's death… they said it was an accident."

Her voice hitched on the words, a mother's grief etched into every syllable. "Now, out of nowhere, they're pinning the murder on Will. I simply don't understand it."

"Murder, as in first-degree murder?" I leaned forward, my eyebrows knitting in disbelief. The clatter of dishes and low hum of conversation around us faded into irrelevance. I could understand third-degree murder, perhaps, because they called it an accident, so there was no intent to kill and no premeditation. Maybe they had discovered that he was there when it happened… when she fell. That, I could possibly understand. But first-degree? That meant they believed he had planned it. Or at least that he meant to kill her. That was way more serious.

"Yes," Diane whispered, her eyes dark pools of torment. "And they won't disclose the new evidence. It's like hitting a wall of silence."

"Will couldn't…." My protest died on my lips, replaced by a hard set to my jaw. "I didn't know him, but I take it you can't fathom him hurting anyone?"

"No. Not in any way." She took a breath, steeling herself. "He was shattered after the accident. I had to take the kids in; he couldn't cope, not then."

"Understandable," I murmured, picturing the broken man she described.

"Eventually, he found his footing again." Diane's face softened with a mixture of pride and sorrow. "Took care of his clinic. He's a pediatrician, Eva Rae—adored by all his little patients and their parents. Ask anyone here, and they'll tell you about his kindness."

"Sounds like a man dedicated to healing, not harming." My thoughts raced, piecing together the image of the man she described.

"Exactly. He's a hero, and Lord knows there aren't many of those around here anymore. On the night he and Angela met, he saved someone's life right in front of her at the wedding they were attending. That's what made Angela fall for him right there on the spot. She would always tell that story… especially to the kids. Always making sure they knew that their dad was a hero." Her voice was fierce now, a lioness defending her kin.

"Speaking of the children, where are they now?" I asked.

"The children are back in California. They've been staying with me since their mother died. Their dad visits as often as he can, but they're better off with me until he fully finds his footing. Now, they're staying with a dear friend while I'm here. But Will… he's lost. Help me, Eva Rae," she whispered, her voice brittle like thin ice. "I don't know where else to turn."

Her fingers trembled slightly as they brushed a napkin, betraying the stoic facade she presented.

"Of course, Diane." My words were soft but firm. "Tell me everything you can. No detail is too small."

"Thank you." The relief in her voice was palpable, a single tear escaping to trace a path down her cheek.

"Will is a good man," I said, more to myself than to

her. "A healer. We'll peel back the layers of this case until we expose the truth."

"Will—he's lost so much already." She dabbed at her eyes with the napkin, fighting to maintain composure.

"Then we'll fight for him," I asserted, my resolve surging like a tide. "Let's start from the beginning, Diane. Anything you remember about the day Angela died, however insignificant it might seem." My voice was low and steady, seeking to ground her amidst the chaos.

She nodded, taking a deep breath, and began to recount the events of that fateful day. As she spoke, each word painted a picture, one I would commit to memory and scrutinize. Every fact was a potential key, every memory a possible clue.

"Will wouldn't harm a fly," Diane insisted, her conviction unshakable. "He's dedicated his life to saving others, not destroying them."

"Someone's made a mistake. Or worse, deliberately pointed the finger at an innocent man," I mused aloud, my mind already sifting through possibilities, motives, and alibis.

"Exactly. He's been framed. I know it."

"Then we'll prove it," I declared, my tone leaving no room for doubt. "I won't rest until we've cleared his name."

Diane's hand reached out, gripping mine with a strength that belied her delicate appearance. At that moment, our partnership was sealed with a shared determination to seek out the truth and restore a family torn apart by tragedy.

"Thank you, Eva Rae," she said, her voice steadier now, fueled by the promise of action.

"Thank me when we're done," I replied, standing up. "Now, let's get to work."

Chapter 8

I pushed through the glass doors of the St. Augustine Police Station, my heart hammering against my ribs. The place reeked of stale coffee and the tang of industrial cleaner, a scent that clung to the walls like an unwelcome ghost. I'd been here before, but never with such a pressing weight on my shoulders.

"I need to see the detective in charge of the Angela Jennings murder case, please," I said, my voice steady despite the gnawing tension inside me. The uniformed officer behind the front desk looked up, his expression flat, bored.

"It's urgent," I added, locking eyes with him. "I need to speak with them now."

"Name?" His question was routine, his fingers poised over the keyboard.

"Agent Eva Rae Thomas," I replied and showed him my badge. "FBI."

The officer led me down a narrow corridor, the walls lined with framed photos of St. Augustine's finest, their smiles almost mocking in the dim fluorescence. He stopped at a door, rapped on it twice, and swung it open without waiting for a reply.

"An Agent Thomas is here to see you," he announced flatly before disappearing back into the hallway.

The office was a claustrophobic den of paperwork mountains and greasy takeout containers. A single bulb flickered above, casting sallow light on the man behind the desk. Detective Mark Larson slouched in his chair, a sneer plastered across his craggy face as if I were the inconvenience of the day. Which I probably was.

"Agent Thomas," I said, pushing the door further ajar. "FBI. I'm here about the Angela Jennings case."

His eyes, bloodshot and ringed with dark circles, barely lifted from the cluttered mess of his desk. He chewed on the end of a pen, a deliberate show of disinterest.

"Jennings?" he grunted, the word laced with derision.

"Working on behalf of Diane Matthews, the victim's mother. Will Jennings' arrest—it doesn't add up." My words cut through the dense air, sharp and insistent.

Larson leaned back, the chair groaning under the shift of weight. He flicked the pen onto the desk, where it rolled aimlessly before coming to rest against a mound of files.

"Ah, the grieving mother-in-law," he drawled, his voice dripping with disdain. "Got the feds to do her dirty work, has she?"

I ignored the jab. "There are gaps in the narrative. We need to ensure we're not overlooking key evidence."

"Key evidence," Larson mimicked, mockery thick in his tone. His gaze finally met mine, and there was something chilling in its vacancy, the lack of empathy or even basic humanity. "You think I don't know how to run an investigation?"

"Collaboration could benefit—" I began, but he cut me off with a snort.

"Look, sweetheart, save your breath. This is my turf. Your badge doesn't impress me."

Larson's chair creaked as he leaned forward, the acrid smell of old sweat wafting across the desk. "Now, if you don't mind, I have actual police work to do."

His dismissal was clear, but I stood my ground, refusing to be intimidated or brushed aside. There was more at stake than his bruised ego.

"Detective Larson," I pressed, keeping my voice cool, "I intend to see this investigation through. With or without your cooperation."

I squared my shoulders, the starched fabric of my shirt scratching slightly as I did so.

I was met with a scoff.

"Detective Larson, you can scoff all you want," I said, meeting his dismissive gaze with a steely one of my own. "But this isn't just about jurisdiction. It's about getting to the truth. And I'm not gonna just stand here and watch as an innocent man goes down for something he didn't do."

"Truth?" He laced his fingers behind his head with an air of ostentatious contempt. "You're out of your depth, Agent Thomas."

"Maybe." My voice was steady, but inside, my pulse raced. "Or maybe I have resources that could help. Diane Matthews is counting on us—on me—to clear her son-in-law's name if he's innocent."

"Resources." He spat the word out like a cherry pit, his sneer deepening. "This department doesn't run on your fancy federal toys."

"Information, Detective." I leaned across the desk, closing the space between us, making it impossible for him to ignore the urgency in my eyes. "That's what I'm asking for."

"Ask away." He flicked an imaginary speck of dust from his sleeve. "Doesn't mean I'll give."

"Someone's future is on the line," I said, refusing to blink first. "Justice demands we look at every angle."

"Justice?" His laugh was a bark, sharp and mocking. "You don't get to lecture me about justice in my own town, Agent Thomas."

"Then prove it." I stood firm, unflinching. "Prove that St. Augustine upholds it. Share the case files with me."

"Share?" He snorted, shaking his head as if I had just told a bad joke. "Dream on."

"Fine." I drew back slowly, knowing when to retreat—for now. "But this isn't over, Detective."

"Sure feels like it from here." Larson's grin was all teeth, zero warmth.

"I just need to know what the new evidence is that has put Jennings in jail," I said.

Larson leaned forward, his elbows digging into the clutter of his desk. "You seem slow on the uptake, Agent Thomas. I'll spell it out for you—no."

"Detective," I countered, keeping my voice steady despite the heat crawling up my neck, "I'm not here to step on toes. I'm here for clarity, for closure."

"Clarity?" His lip curled. "You're clouding up my precinct with your Fed badge and big words. This is local police business."

"Local or not, a man's life hangs in the balance. We have to get this right."

"Right," he echoed, mockery lacing his tone. "And you think you've got the monopoly on that?"

"Detective Larson," I leaned in, my voice steady, "think about the victim's family. He has children. They'll be left without parents if he's put away. A fresh set of eyes might be beneficial."

"Beneficial?" He snorted, his arms folded like a fortress wall. "Or bureaucratic?"

"Both of us want the same thing," I insisted. "A swift resolution."

"Swift and sloppy don't mix." The words slithered out with disdain.

"Accuracy is key—and I can help with that."

"Help?" His laugh was a barbed wire. "You're more of a hindrance."

"Detective—"

"Save it." He turned away, rifling through papers on his cluttered desk, dismissal written in every crease of his uniform.

I paused. My next words were caught in my throat, left unsaid. He wouldn't budge. It was evident in the rigid line of his back, the way his fingers twitched to shoo me away again.

"Fine." It came out sharper than intended. A mental pivot was needed, and fast.

I didn't let my gaze waver as I backed toward the door, dissecting the room with each step. Bookshelves lined with binders, a computer buzzing on standby.

"Thank you, Detective," I said, though gratitude was the furthest thing from my heart. "Your cooperation has been… noted."

"Note this." He pointed at the door without looking up. "Don't let it hit you on the way out."

My hand found the doorknob, cold and unyielding—a reflection of the man before me. I paused. I took a deep breath, refusing to be cowed by his dismissive posture.

"Is there someone else I can speak with?" I asked, each word measured and clear. "Perhaps another detective who has been on the case?"

The smirk that crawled across his face was like a shadow passing over sun-warmed sand.

"Oh, Agent Thomas," he drawled, the sarcasm dripping from his voice like molasses. "This isn't some open house where you shop around for cooperation."

His fingers danced mockingly on the cluttered desk, tapping out a silent rhythm only he could hear.

"You want the files? Go through the proper channels. Fill out your forms, get your clearances, and stand in line."

"That's gonna take too long. I don't have that kind of time," I said. "The trial is coming up soon."

Heat flushed my cheeks, but I refused to let it reach my eyes. They remained cool, green pools of determination.

"Not really my problem, is it?"

I turned, leaving him alone with his victory smirk and festering office, the door closing on the sound of his chuckle.

My mind raced through regulations and statutes as I made my way out of the precinct, already plotting my next move. There was more than one way to peel an orange, and I'd peel this case wide open.

Chapter 9

THEN:

Will guided Angela through the labyrinth of the city park, where ancient oaks and whispering pines cast intricate shadows on the winding path. Their fingers were interlocked, a silent testament to the unspoken connection that hummed between them and had for a long time while dating. The sun played peekaboo through the leaves, dappling Angela's blonde hair with flickers of gold.

"It's a perfect day, isn't it?" Angela breathed in the scent of fresh grass and blooming flowers.

"Couldn't agree more," Will replied, his voice steady yet laced with an undercurrent of anticipation that only nature's chorus could hear.

The further they ventured, the less they encountered other souls until only the distant laughter of children and the occasional chirp of a bird accompanied their solitude. Angela's eyes danced with curiosity as Will led her off the main path, steering her toward a secluded glen that seemed untouched by time.

"Where are we going?" she asked, a playful challenge in her tone.

"Somewhere special," Will responded, a tightness in his throat betraying the momentous weight of his intentions.

They arrived at a clearing, embraced on all sides by a fortress of greenery. Here, the sunlight was bold and assertive, claiming the space as its own. Angela looked around, her face the picture of serene beauty framed by nature's canvas.

Will's heart hammered against his ribcage. He released her hand and dropped to one knee, his movements deliberate. He produced a small box from his pocket, feeling its weight like destiny in his palm.

"Angela Matthews," he began, his voice a soft but firm anchor in the breeze, "I've loved you since the moment I saw you."

The ring emerged from its velvet cocoon, catching the sunlight and transforming it into a thousand tiny rainbows. Angela gasped, a delicate hand covering her mouth, her eyes reflecting the sparkles thrown by the diamond.

"Will you marry me?" Will's words hung in the air, tender and hopeful, the silence around them thick with promise.

Angela's breath caught, suspended in a moment that stretched and twisted time. Her eyes, vast oceans of azure, widened as the reality of Will's question sank into her heart like a stone breaking the surface of a still pond. She nodded, words unnecessary in the face of such raw emotion.

"More than anything," she finally managed, her voice a whisper that carried the weight of all their shared dreams. "Yes. The answer is yes."

Will leaped to his feet, the ring now a symbol of their intertwined futures. He slipped it onto her finger—a perfect fit—and they both stared for a heartbeat, marveling at how a small band of gold could hold so much promise.

"Angela," he breathed out, and she met his gaze, finding a reflection of her own overwhelming joy.

"Will," she replied, the name a vow in itself.

Their lips met then, a collision of passion and certitude that marked the beginning of a lifetime. This kiss was a seal, an unspoken pledge that bound them closer than any words could. It was a fiery crescendo that rose from the depths of their beings, a confluence of every whispered "I love you" that had danced between them in the quiet of night.

Around them, the world blurred into irrelevance, the park with its towering trees and dappled sunlight fading into a backdrop for two souls fusing into one. There was only the sensation of connection, the electric charge that hummed through their joined hands, the soft sounds of their unity that spoke louder than any cheer.

They parted their lips, breathless but undefeated by the intensity. Their foreheads touched, a silent communion as they allowed the world to spin back into focus, their shared pulse the rhythm to which it moved.

THE GRAVEL CRUNCHED under Will's shoes as they approached the Matthews' family home later that same day. Angela's hand, still trembling with fresh excitement, gripped his tightly.

"Ready?" he whispered, a conspiratorial glint in his eyes.

"Let's do this," Angela said, her voice a mix of nerves and delight.

The door swung open before they could knock. A swell of cheers erupted as faces familiar and dear crowded the entryway. Angela's heart leaped into her throat, her breath stolen by the sudden wave of affection. They stepped over the threshold together, enveloped in the warm embrace of their awaiting world.

"Congratulations!" The chorus of joyous exclamations washed over them like a celebratory tide.

"Angela, my darling!" Her aunt's voice rose above the rest, the woman's arms encircling her in a fierce hug that left no room for anything but the moment.

Glasses clinked, held aloft by hands interlinked by blood and bond. Will's arm found its way around Angela's waist, grounding her as she floated on the sea of elation that filled the room.

"To Angela and Will," her uncle called out, his glass raised high, a beacon for all to follow. "To love that endures!"

"To love that endures!" The echo rang true, bouncing off walls adorned with memories.

Will's gaze met hers, steady and sure. In his eyes, she saw her world, her future. Smiles spread, laughter bubbled, and Angela's gentle voice lifted to join the symphony of good wishes.

"Thank you," she beamed, her soul alight. "Thank you all."

Diane's arms swept around Angela, a fortress of maternal love. Her tears cascaded, diamonds of joy against the dusk. Angela's breath hitched, her own eyes shimmering in response.

"Mom…," she whispered, voice muffled in the warmth of Diane's embrace.

"It's your dream come true," Diane said through tears, "it's what you've always wanted, my dear."

Angela nodded, words unnecessary in the current of understanding that flowed between them.

"And what a handsome man he is," she added. "And a doctor. You're a lucky girl. Don't ruin this."

"I won't, Mom. I promise."

"Will!" His older brother's voice boomed across the gathering, slicing through the hum of conversation. He approached with outstretched hands, clasping Will's with a vigor that underlined his words. "You did it. You got the girl, and you've made us all proud today."

"Thank you, " Will replied.

The evening unfolded like a series of snapshots: smiles exchanged, glasses raised, stories spun into the growing tapestry of their lives together. Will and Angela wove through the crowd, threads of gold in a familial fabric.

A YEAR LATER, sunlight pierced the stained glass, casting kaleidoscopic patterns on the aisle. Angela glided forward, her gown a cascade of silk and lace that whispered against the floor with each step. Her father had died years ago, so it was her uncle who gave her away on this happy day. Her gaze was anchored ahead, where Will stood—a beacon of calm and certainty.

"Beautiful," someone murmured as she passed.

The word seemed too small for what this moment held—too simple for the swell of emotion that tightened around Angela's heart like a vise. She could feel every eye in the church, but they might as well have been miles away.

There was only Will, his smile reaching out to her, promising everything.

"Angela Matthews," the officiant began, his voice deep and resonant, "do you take William Jennings to be your lawfully wedded husband?"

Her breath hitched. "I do."

"And do you, William, take Angela to be your lawfully wedded wife?"

Will's voice didn't waver. "I do."

Vows were spoken, a lifetime condensed into sentences. The rings, cool and heavy with significance, slipped onto their fingers—a tangible symbol of the intangible bond they shared.

"By the power vested in me…"

The words faded into a crescendo of anticipation. Angela's pulse hammered a against her throat, her fingers trembling slightly as they found Will's.

"…I now pronounce you husband and wife."

A collective exhale swept through the congregation like a wave cresting and breaking over them. Tears blurred Angela's vision but couldn't obscure the sight of Will, her anchor, her now-husband.

"Kiss the bride."

Their lips met, a collision of love and destiny. The kiss was a seal, an agreement made not just in front of witnesses but in the silent language of their hearts—a conversation that had started the day they met and would continue for all the days to come.

Applause erupted, loud and joyous. Angela's mother shed a tear as they turned to face the world, hand in hand, united. Angela's eyes flickered across the crowd, catching glimpses of tear-streaked cheeks and wide smiles. This was more than a ceremony; it was the beginning of a journey—one they would walk together, step by step, through whatever life might bring.

"Mrs. and Mr. Jennings," someone called out, the titles new and exhilarating.

"Forever starts now," Will whispered, his voice for her alone.

"Forever," she echoed, her heart surging with the weight and wonder of that single word.

Chapter 10

I paced, the Airbnb's unfamiliar patterned rug scratching the soles of my feet. Three steps forward, pivot, and three steps back. My jaw clenched with each turn, a metronome of frustration. The room was too small, or maybe it was just me feeling too large, too full of restless energy that demanded action.

I stopped mid-stride, glaring at the phone on the coffee-stained table. It mocked me with its silent, static black screen. Enough. I snatched it up, the device cold and unyielding in my palm. The screen lit up to my touch, fingers punching it with a rapid-fire tap-tap-tap. Matt's number. His name blinked on the display, a beacon in the dimly lit room.

"Come on," I muttered under my breath, the phone pressed against my ear, the ringing tone echoing like a siren in the dense silence. Each ring twisted my gut tighter, a coiled spring waiting to snap.

He picked up.

"Hey, Matt. How are the kids?" My voice wavered

between the lines, betraying a mother's longing disguised as casual inquiry.

"Good, Eva. Christine didn't make it to school today, but there's always tomorrow," Matt's words floated through the phone, his tone even, carrying a hint of forced cheerfulness that created a subtle barrier between us.

"How's Alex? Is he still on track for team captain?"

"Tryouts went well. He's optimistic." His responses were succinct and steady—like droplets in a leak, not quite enough to quench my thirst for connection.

"And Angel?" I pressed, my heart squeezing with each word, picturing her tiny hands and bright eyes, worlds away from this sterile room.

"Angel's... she's missing you. Keeps asking when Mommy's coming home." The distance in Matt's voice seemed to shrink for a moment, a shared ache bridging the miles.

"Hey, how's the case coming along?" Matt finally shifted the topic, his voice carrying the weight of both curiosity and concern.

I exhaled, feeling the pressure in my chest release. "It's... complicated," I began, pacing again, my footsteps tapping a rhythm on the wooden floor. "There's an innocent man sitting in a cell, and every second counts."

"Sounds serious," he said, the rustle of fabric hinting he'd leaned forward, engaged despite himself.

"More than you know. The evidence is confidential; all I know is that it's a witness statement, but without the case files, I'm chasing shadows." My fingers traced the grain of the dining table, my mind racing. "I need those files, Matt. Do you think that you...?"

"No, Eva Rae. Absolutely not."

"You're the only one I know who can access them quickly enough."

"No, Eva Rae—"

"Please. I don't have enough time," I cut him off before he could articulate the risks he would be taking, the urgency leaving no room for doubt. "This man's life and his future hang in the balance. And we both know what's at stake here."

There was a pause on the line, and when he spoke, his words came out slow, weighted.

"Eva Rae, this could blow up in our faces. My job—"

"Your job can't be more important than an innocent man's life." I shot back, halting mid-pace to lean against the wall, feeling the cool paint against my forehead.

"Of course, it isn't, but—" His voice cracked with conflict, "I just got this desk position, Eva. I love it. Finally, I found something I can do and love to do. After everything… I can't afford to lose it."

"Matt, remember why we do this?" I urged, my plea slicing through the silence that followed his words. "For the people with no one else to fight for them."

"I know, I do, but—"

"No 'buts,' Matt. This is who we are. Who you are." The intensity in my voice rose like a tide as I pushed off the wall, striding back into motion. "A lifeline for those sinking in a sea rigged against them."

"Damn it, Eva Rae…."

He let out a long sigh, and I could almost see him running a hand through his sandy blond hair, the gesture of frustration so uniquely his.

"Think of Angel," I said softly, invoking our daughter's name—a name that symbolized our bond, our shared ideals. "We're shaping the world she inherits. What if, one day, she looks up at us and asks what we did when we had the power to make a difference?"

His silence was telling. It stretched out, filled only by the sound of my own breaths, quick and shallow.

"Okay," he finally murmured, the word laced with resignation and the unmistakable undercurrent of the courage I knew so well. "Okay, Eva Rae. I'll do it. But you'll owe me."

"Thank you," I whispered, relief flooding through me as I ended the call, my fingers trembling slightly as they brushed over the phone screen. It was a small victory in a larger battle, and with Matt now alongside me, the odds just might have tipped in our favor.

At least, I hoped so.

Chapter 11

I swiped my ID at the jail's entrance, the beep louder than my thudding pulse. Metal doors clanked open, and I stepped inside the cold, a sharp contrast from the humid air of St. Augustine that clung to my skin only moments before. The guard gave me a nod, familiar with my face but never easing on protocol.

"Empty your pockets," he instructed, his voice as cold as the steel table before me.

Keys. Badge. Phone. Gum wrapper. Each item landed with a clink or a soft thud. They slid my belongings aside and waved me through the metal detector. It squawked approval, and I gathered my things, shoving them back into my pockets.

"Follow me," said another uniform, leading me down the sterile corridor. Fluorescent lights hummed overhead, flickering in rhythm with each step I took. My ponytail swayed, red strands catching the light like threads of fire.

Will Jennings was there behind the glass partition, his eyes two dark pools in a face carved with worry. I had seen that look before—on victims, families, and anyone touched by tragedy. But Will's despair was etched deeper; it came from being accused of the very tragedy that had shattered him.

I sat, lifting the receiver, our reflections mingling on the glass.

"Agent Thomas," he said, his voice barely carrying through the phone line. "Diane said she thought you might come."

"Mr. Jennings. Will." My reply was steady, a counterpoint to the drumbeat in my chest. His fingers twitched, a visible echo of the turmoil within.

"Thanks for coming," he said, the words fighting their way out.

"Of course." I exhaled slowly, scanning his face for any sign of deceit, finding nothing but raw pain. The chair was cold against my skin as I leaned in, mirroring his posture of defeat with one of unwavering support.

"How are you holding up?"

"Okay, I guess," Will said, a tremor in his voice betraying the calm he attempted to portray. His hands fumbled with the edges of his orange jumpsuit. "I'm here, aren't I?"

"Tell me," I said, my gaze fixed on his, willing him to draw strength from my resolve. "About the night when it happened."

"It was Danny…," he started, his eyes darting away before finding mine again. "That's our son. He screamed, and I have never heard a scream like that before. It went straight through my bones."

"Go on," I urged, my heart hammering with each beat, a metronome ticking down the seconds we had left.

"His screams tore through the night." Will's voice shook as he continued. "I've never heard him like that—pure terror."

My breath hitched, but I kept my face composed, a blank canvas for him to paint his nightmare upon.

"Take me there," I said, my voice a command more than a request. "Where were you?"

"I was asleep. In bed. I thought Angela was sleeping next to me. But she must have gotten up… for whatever reason, I don't know. Maybe she needed water? Maybe she couldn't sleep? I don't know. I was sound asleep when I heard my son's screams. It was awful. I jumped out of bed and ran toward the sound. Every step echoed like a drumbeat." Will's eyes were distant, reliving the nightmare. "Those seconds… they stretched into eternity."

"Then?" My question was sharp, a knife edge to slice through the haze of his memory.

"I found her…." His voice was a thread, fraying. "She was just lying there. So still. Angela…."

"Did you touch her? Check for a pulse?"

"I did; there was a pulse. My hands… they were shaking." He closed his eyes, squeezing the image out. "I couldn't… think."

"Will, focus." I leaned closer, narrowing the space between us. "The call—tell me about the call."

"The phone slipped twice out of my hand." Frustration seeped through his creased brow. "Third time, I got it. Dialed 911."

"Exact words?"

"Help… need help. My wife, she's not moving." Will's voice cracked anew, splintered by the weight of that moment. "She fell. I told them she had fallen. I'm pretty sure. I don't remember it exactly. It's all a blur."

"That's understandable. What did they say the response time was?"

"It would be fast, they said. That's all, I believe. But it

didn't feel fast at all; each tick of the clock—was like a hammer on my skull."

"And you stayed with her?"

"Every second until sirens cut through the silence." He inhaled sharply as if the wail of the ambulance was right there in the room with us. "The pulse disappeared, and I did CPR until they got there. They took over, and she came back to life. She was still alive when they left with her. But she… she never made it to the hospital. Died in the ambulance. I never… never got to say goodbye. I should have gone with her in the ambulance, but then what about the children? I had to stay behind with them and bring them with me. But yes, I did everything I could until the very end."

"Good." I nodded, filing away each word, each inflection. "That's good, Will."

His hands trembled like a sparrow caught in a storm.

"Hey," I whispered, the word a lifeline thrown across the chasm of his despair. "You're doing good. I know this isn't easy."

Will's eyes captured mine, twin pools of pain.

"We had plans, Eva Rae." The dam broke; words were now spilling out with his tears. "A vacation to Barcelona, we were going to take dance lessons… salsa, for the wedding anniversary. We had ten years coming up."

"Sounds beautiful," I murmured.

"Angela…" His voice was shredded, raw, and bleeding. "She was… everything. She was all I had. Her laughter was the best, her laughter—it filled rooms." His chest heaved, a silent sob fighting its way free. "Now, there's just silence. I try to remember what her laughter sounded like, but it's getting harder and harder."

"Keep going." I prodded, not unkindly.

"Her dreams, they were big. So damn big." Salty trails carved paths down his cheeks. "Our future—it was stolen."

"Stolen," I echoed, a vow etched within the single word.

I blinked hard, the sheen of tears threatening to spill over. "Will," I started, my voice steady despite the storm raging inside, "I'm on your side. I believe you're telling the truth. But I needed to see for myself and look into your eyes to be certain."

He met my gaze, his own eyes red-rimmed and haunted.

"Every clue, every witness," I continued, "I'll chase them down. No rock left unturned."

"Thank you," he managed, his voice a hoarse whisper.

"Talk to me about Angela," I said, shifting gears. "Help me know her—the real her, not just what's on paper."

For a moment, there was only the buzz of the fluorescent lights overhead, then Will's face softened, a faint smile blossoming through the grief as he remembered.

"Angela had this… energy." The word tumbled out, tinged with warmth. "She'd walk into a room, and it was like suddenly everything was brighter, more alive."

"Sounds like she was remarkable," I noted, my mind painting a picture of a woman full of life and light, now reduced to cold case files and whispers behind closed doors.

"More than you know," Will sighed, and he launched into a story about Angela, one Halloween when she dressed up as a superhero to surprise their son. His laughter, rare and precious, echoed against the concrete walls, a brief respite from the despair.

"Her spirit," he said, wiping away fresh tears, "it's what we need to remember."

"Her spirit will guide us," I assured him, feeling the

truth of it deep in my bones. Angela wasn't just a victim; she was the heartbeat of this investigation.

"Have the police mentioned anything about what they have on you? What new evidence has come up?" I asked.

"Nope. Not a word."

"Do you suspect foul play in your wife's death? Would anyone have reason to want her dead?" I asked.

"Like who? No! My wife was the nicest person alive. Everyone loved her…." he paused. "Wait, she did have problems with our neighbor, Carol. She thought she flirted with me and confronted her about it once. But that's all. Those two hated one another."

"Enough for murder?"

He hesitated. "I don't know about that."

I nodded, noting it on my pad. "Anyone else? Former colleagues? She didn't work, did she?"

"Not anymore. She used to be a teacher, but all the kids loved her, and so did the other teachers, so no, I can't think of anything there."

Our time was up. The guard let me know. I pushed back my chair, the metal legs scraping against the linoleum with a jarring screech.

"I'll fight for you, Will," I said, the words heavy like lead yet fierce with promise. "We will get to the bottom of this."

"Thank you," he whispered, his voice barely rising above a murmur. The skin around his eyes crinkled, a dam holding back a reservoir of anguish. "For believing in me… for everything."

The intensity in his gaze struck a chord, igniting a fire that coursed through my veins—every fiber of my being vibrated with the weight of the responsibility. I nodded once, firmly.

"I won't rest, Will. Not until the world sees what we see."

"Angela would've liked you," he said, the lines on his face softening for a breath, revealing the man he used to be before grief wore him down.

"Then I'm honored," I replied, feeling the ghost of Angela's presence, a whisper urging us forward.

I brushed the wetness from my cheeks, fingertips grazing over skin that felt too tight, too raw. Standing tall, I met Will's gaze one last time before parting.

"You'll hear from me soon," I said, voice steady despite the storm of emotion.

"Thank you, Eva Rae," he replied, the words barely above a whisper but carrying the weight of his world.

Turning on my heel, I strode from the visiting area. The pieces lay scattered in my mind—a jigsaw puzzle begging for order. Facts interweaved with hunches, timelines intersecting with alibis. My pulse hammered against my temples, urgency seeping into my veins like adrenaline.

Angela's memory haunted the periphery of my thoughts, a silent siren calling me back to duty. There were answers out there, shrouded in shadows and half-truths, and I would unearth them. For Will. For Angela.

The metal door clanged shut behind me, its echo a dull thud in my chest. My feet found the rhythm of duty as I navigated the sterile corridor, each step an anchor dragging me forward. The deputy at the security checkpoint gave a curt nod, his face an unreadable mask. I returned the gesture without missing a beat.

Outside, the Florida sun was unforgiving, a spotlight on the path laid out before me. I squinted against the glare, shielding my eyes with a hand still trembling from the visit's intensity. The heat wrapped around me, oppressive, as if trying to smother the fire inside. I kept thinking... if it had been me. If I had lost Matt and now was accused of having killed him? The thought was beyond devastating.

"Someone's gotta fight for him," I whispered, the mantra propelling me across the jail's parking lot. Gravel crunched beneath my shoes, a staccato accompaniment to the rapid drumming of my heart. I could taste the bitterness of the task ahead and was worried I would fail, but there was no going back now.

The car door slammed with conviction, sealing me inside. My fingers danced over the steering wheel. The engine roared to life with a twist of the key, a beast awakened and hungry for the hunt.

"Time's ticking," I muttered, throwing the car into gear.

I gunned the accelerator, the vehicle lurching forward like a hound unleashed. There were leads to chase down, witnesses to press, and evidence to reexamine. Each moment was precious, each clue a potential lifeline.

I drove on, relentless.

Chapter 12

THEN:

Angela sat at the kitchen table, her fingers tracing the grain of the wood, gaze fixed on Will. He stirred his coffee, lost in a mechanical rhythm that seemed to echo the ticking of the wall clock—relentless, monotonous.

They had been married for five years, and she had given birth to two children. But lately, something had changed.

"Will?" Her voice sliced through the silence, a tremble betraying her calm exterior.

He glanced up, spoon clinking against the mug's edge. "Hmm?"

"Is everything okay?" The words barely took shape, laced with worry. "Are we okay?"

In the space between heartbeats, Will's eyes flicked away. Guilt? Maybe. He set the spoon down and forced a casual shrug.

"Yes, everything is okay. Why wouldn't it be?"

"You've been... distant lately. You barely say anything to me."

He shook his head, then got up and put his cup in the sink. "It's just work stuff. And speaking of, I should be going now if I want to make it to my morning meeting." He pecked her on the cheek, then left.

Her throat tightened. Lies didn't suit him. But she exhaled, smoothing out the creases on the linen tablecloth, choosing trust over suspicion... for now.

After Will left, Angela paced the kitchen. She paused at the window, peering out as if the answer might be etched in the frosty glass. The doorbell's chime cut through her reverie, and she hastened to welcome solace in human form.

"Mom," Angela exhaled as Diane stepped into the embrace of the coolness of the AC in the kitchen.

"Darling," Diane greeted, her presence an instant balm to the room's chill. "Sweet tea sounds perfect."

They settled at the table, silence stretching between them, laden with words unspoken. Diane poured the iced tea, then handed a glass to her with a deep sigh.

"What's going on?" Diane asked, tilting her head. "I sense something is wrong with you. Is it the kids?"

"Mom," Angela began, voice barely above a whisper, "there's something... off with Will."

Diane offered a smile, the practiced curve of her lips contrasting the furrowed concern on Angela's brow. With a touch, light as a petal, she reached across the table, her fingers grazing Angela's hand.

"Every marriage dances through shadows, my dear," Diane soothed, her tone wrapping Angela in a shawl of maternal wisdom. "It's natural. Especially when you have children. They take up a lot of space and exhaust their

DARK LITTLE SERETCS

parents. There really isn't a lot of energy left once the day is over. It'll get better when they're older."

Angela felt the weight of her mother's gaze, heavy with years of unspoken understanding. Yet beneath it, an undercurrent of dismissal pulled at her, eroding the shores of her resolve. Her heart ached, a silent plea for recognition hovering in the air, unanswered.

Angela's hand clenched around her tea, the glass a fragile barrier against the rising tide of her worries.

"He's distant, Mom. It's been going on for a while now."

"It's probably just work, honey," her mom said. "Men get like that. Exactly how is he distant?"

"He forgot our anniversary, and he dismisses conversations about the kids," she said, the words tumbling out like runaway beads from a snapped necklace.

Diane's brows knit together briefly, her elegant posture shifting in the cushioned chair.

"Angela, love... I hardly think that qualifies as"

"His phone is always locked. And there are nights when he comes home late, reeking of someone else's perfume." Angela's voice cracked, the fear and determination mingling into a tremulous force. "I'm sure of it."

A flicker of concern danced across Diane's features. She leaned forward, her eyes searching Angela's face as if looking for the daughter she once knew, who saw the world in softer hues.

"Sweetheart," Diane began with a note of caution, "are you certain you're not just... spinning tales?"

Tears pooled in Angela's eyes, blurring the kitchen into a watercolor smear. "Mom, please."

"Think of all Will's done for you. His work is demanding, and—" Diane's voice was a velvet cover, trying to smooth the creases in her daughter's narrative.

"Mom, it's not just stress. There are messages he hides from me!" Angela's plea scattered the veil of calm Diane tried to weave. "He will turn his phone away as I approach him or put it down suddenly."

Diane reached out, her touch light on Angela's trembling hands, her own heart caught in the snare of maternal instinct.

"Darling, you know Will. He loves you."

"Does he?" Angela whispered, the question a splinter in her chest.

"Of course," Diane insisted, but her voice lacked its usual conviction, her glance briefly flitting away before settling back on Angela's distraught face.

The room seemed to contract around them, the air thick with the weight of unspoken fears and uncertainty.

Angela's fingers clenched into fists, nails digging crescents into her palms. She drew a deep breath, the air seemingly reluctant to enter her lungs.

"Mom," she said, voice steadying like iron forged in fire, "I need you to listen to me—really listen."

Diane's posture shifted, a fortress of resistance waning. Her eyes, once guarded, softened under Angela's earnest gaze. "I am listening, Angie. I've been listening all this time."

"Will is hiding things from me, and I can feel it eating away at me every day." Each word Angela spoke was deliberate and measured, carving out her reality. "It's more than just missed dinners or distant looks. I'm scared, Mom."

The confession hung between them, heavy and undeniable. Diane's hand fluttered to her chest where a gold locket lay—a relic she had inherited from her own mother.

"Angela," Diane began, her voice now a whisper betraying inner turmoil, "If that's what's going on, then you need to figure out what you want to do about it."

"I don't know how—" Angela started, but the question died on her lips. The admission was a gut punch, her worst fears inching toward truth.

"Confrontation has never been our way, has it?" Diane's eyes flickered with something ancient, a history of untold stories.

"No," Angela agreed, her response a mirror of recognition. "But silence hasn't protected us either, has it? I mean, Dad cheated, didn't he? I remember you telling me about it. That's why you two divorced before he died."

Diane's face, usually an unreadable canvas, crumpled slightly at the edges. "No, darling. Perhaps not. I will say that I've also noticed him being a little distant the past few times I've been over here for dinner. I don't want to jump to conclusions as it could be many things. But I understand your worry."

Angela's heart, already leaden, sank deeper into the abyss of doubt and fear. If Diane had noticed, then the veil of normalcy they'd clung to was nothing but thin threads, ready to tear.

"Thank you," Angela whispered, the words a lifeline thrown across the chasm growing within her family. "For seeing it too."

THE FRONT DOOR clicked shut behind Diane. Angela lingered on the porch, watching as her mother's car pulled away, the hum of the engine fading into the evening air. Their eyes had locked moments before, a silent exchange that spoke volumes; she could trust her mother's support; they were in this together now.

Angela turned, her gaze falling upon the house that once promised perpetual sanctuary. Now, it whispered secrets. She steeled herself, her jaw set, and crossed the threshold with a deliberateness that echoed through the empty hallway.

Inside, the quiet was a living thing, pulsing with the heartbeat of the unknown. She allowed herself a moment, just one, to feel the weight of her resolve settle into her bones. Then, she moved.

Her steps were measured and determined as she ascended the staircase. Each creak of the wooden steps matched the rhythm of her quickening pulse. At the top, she paused, hand resting on the cool banister, and drew a deep breath. This was strategic warfare within her own walls, and she needed a plan.

In the sanctuary of their bedroom, Angela paced, her thoughts a whirlwind of strategy and suspicion. She opened a drawer, fingers brushing over Will's neatly folded shirts, and closed it again. Too obvious.

"Think," she muttered to herself.

She visualized Will's daily routines, his habits, and the slight deviations that had begun to form an unsettling pattern. The late-night phone calls he dismissed with a wave, the unexplained absences, the receipts from local restaurants left carelessly in his pockets—a trail if one knew how to look.

Her eyes fell upon his study, a room filled with the musk of old books and leather—a place where he spent hours under the guise of work. It was there she would start her search. A surge of adrenaline propelled her forward.

"Carefully," she reminded herself.

At the study door, Angela's hand hesitated on the knob. Her heart hammered against her ribs like a prisoner seeking escape. She pushed the door open.

"You need to know. You need to find out the truth," she whispered into the silence.

With meticulous precision, Angela began her quest. She hurried to the computer and turned it on. She checked his emails but found nothing, then checked the internet search history—only to find it scrubbed clean.

She stared at it, startled.

"Who cleans their internet history if they don't have anything to hide?" she noted with a frown.

A floorboard creaked somewhere, the sudden sound slicing through the tense atmosphere. Angela froze, her breath caught in her throat. Was it Will? No, it was way too early. Still, caution was her ally.

She turned off the computer, ensuring everything was as Will had left it. She backed out of the room, her movements fluid and silent, a dance of necessity.

"Tomorrow," she thought, "another day, another chance to uncover what's hidden."

Angela closed the study door with a soft click, her mind already racing ahead. Plans layered upon plans, each step bringing her closer to either salvation or ruin.

"Ready," she affirmed, a whisper lost in the shadows. "For whatever you're hiding, Will."

Chapter 13

The ping of my inbox sliced through the stillness of the room. I lunged for the mouse, clicking with a ferocity that betrayed my calm exterior. Matt's name flashed on the screen, and the subject line simply read "Case Files." My heart hammered as I opened the email, downloading the attachment without a second's hesitation.

"Come on; come on," I muttered to myself, the progress bar inching along as if wading through molasses. When the files finally bloomed open on my computer, I wasted no time in diving into the digital depths.

Images cascaded across the screen, each crime scene photo a macabre jigsaw piece waiting to be fitted into place. My eyes narrowed, the world around me fading until there was nothing but the task at hand. A shattered floor vase lay like a fractured skull on the hardwood floor; I could almost hear the echoes of it breaking as Angela knocked it over when ending her days at the bottom of the stairs.

Photo after photo scrolled past, my mouse wheel squeaking slightly under the pressure of my thumb. A glass with a lipstick stain that spoke of hurried sips taken perhaps amidst an argument.

"Interesting," I exhaled softly, leaning closer to the monitor. I noticed a faint smudge on the doorframe to the bedroom. I filled my notepad with scribbles, arrows pointing from one observation to another, forming a roadmap of disorder and desperation.

The images conjured questions that buzzed in my mind like hornets. Where was the struggle? What secrets did the silent walls keep? I dissected every shadow and reflection, searching for that elusive thread that would unravel the truth.

My focus never wavered as I cataloged each anomaly, each inconsistency. Time ceased to exist, measured only by the growing list of notes before me. There was a story here, woven within these digital frames, and I was determined to read between the pixels.

The cursor blinked on the screen like a heartbeat, persistent and rhythmic. I clicked on the video file labeled "Interview – Carol Rudolph" and watched as the scene unfolded, Carol's living room coming into focus behind her. She was perched on the edge of an antique sofa, her fingers laced tightly in her lap. She was about six or seven years younger than Angela had been. Good looking, too. Beautiful even.

"Ms. Carol Rudolph," the off-screen interviewer began, and I leaned forward, eyes narrowing as I studied her every micro-expression. There was something about the way her gaze darted to the left, how her lips pressed into a thin line when Angela's name came up. The calibration of my instincts told me there was more beneath her words, and I trusted that gut feeling like a lifeline.

"Everything was fine until Angela moved in," Carol said, her voice a touch too casual. But the flicker of anger in her eyes, quickly masked, caught my attention. "That's when everything changed around here. She never liked me. I was friends with Will long before they got married. He bought the house almost the same time I did mine, with the money I had inherited from my parents when they died. Will and I would hang out all the time before he married her. I barely ever saw him after that. She wouldn't allow it."

I paused the video, taking a moment to let the insight simmer. This video wasn't going to be enough. It was time for a face-to-face conversation.

Chapter 14

Carol's house stood like a watchful guardian over her manicured lawn, the exterior a stark white against the Florida sun. My knock echoed through the still air, a prelude to the undercurrent of tension I already felt brewing.

"Can I help you?" Carol answered the door with a cautious smile, but it didn't quite reach her eyes.

"Eva Rae Thomas, FBI. I have some questions about Angela Jennings."

A flicker of discomfort ran across her face.

"Of course," she replied, though her pause was telling. I stepped inside, taking in the pristine condition of her home. Porcelain figurines lined the shelves, each positioned just so, reflective of a life ordered down to the millimeter.

"Mind if we sit?" I gestured to the same antique sofa from the video, its floral pattern now registering as overly bright.

"Please." Her voice held a hint of reluctance, and she smoothed her skirt as she sat, creating a barrier of fabric between us.

"Will mentioned you had issues with Angela," I started direct, not softening the blow.

"Ah, that. It was nothing, really. Small things," she countered quickly, eyes fixed on a point past my shoulder. "She complained about me playing loud music and having late-night visitors. Nothing major."

"Nothing that would cause you to hold a grudge?" My question hung in the air like humidity, thick and unrelenting.

"Absolutely not," Carol retorted, but her hands betrayed her, clenching into fists then releasing. "Angela and I were civil to one another."

"Yet Will thinks differently," I pressed, tilting my head slightly, observing as her posture stiffened. "He almost made me convinced there's more to the story."

"Will is," she hesitated, swallowing hard, "mistaken."

"Or perhaps he saw something you wish he hadn't." I leaned in closer, watching as her facade cracked, the strain etched deep in her furrowed brow.

"Are you implying something, Agent Thomas?" Carol's voice rose, a sharp note of defensiveness slicing through the calm.

"No. Just asking questions," I smiled. "It's my job."

Carol's gaze darted, a sparrow trapped in a room too small. "I've told the police everything," she insisted, voice quavering like a plucked string.

"Everything?" I pressed, senses tuned to the tremble in her words and the way her eyes flickered away from mine.

"Yes—yes." A breath hitched in her throat, a silent alarm bell.

"Unconvincing," I whispered under my breath. Carol's shoulders tensed, a telltale sign.

"Excuse me?"

"Did you ever spend time with Angela? Meet up with

her alone?" I asked. "Or were you only interested in talking to Will and being with him?"

"Listen, Agent. I heard your little comment just now, and I don't appreciate it. I have been nice and entertained you and your little quest here, but this is the end of it. I would like for you to leave. Now."

I stared at her. I had hit a nerve, no doubt about it.

"Now," she repeated.

There was nothing more I could do. I stood to my feet. She had told me more than she thought.

"Well, thank you for your time."

Outside, the Florida sun blazed, indifferent to the drama unfolding within. I drove back to the Airbnb, the weight of suspicion heavy on my shoulders. The place was quiet, too quiet.

Opening the case files again, I sifted through facts and testimonies, searching for the thread that would unravel Carol's story. The phone rang, splintering the silence. Olivia's face filled the screen on Facetime.

"Hey, Mom."

"Hi, honey." My heart clenched with longing. "How are things?"

"Usual chaos." Her laughter was a balm to my soul. "Alex scored a goal today! And he won't stop talking about it."

"Did he?" A smile found its way through my concern. Then it froze as I realized I had missed it. Again. "That's amazing."

"Mom?" Christine's voice cut in, worry etched into every syllable. "When are you coming home?"

"Soon, baby," I lied, not knowing if it held any truth. "Soon."

The call ended, leaving me submerged in the silence of

my temporary quarters, the absence of my children echoing louder than ever.

Back to the files, I forced focus, determined to peel back the layers of deceit before time betrayed us all.

The cursor blinked on the screen, a steady rhythm against the chaos of my mind. I scanned the digital case file, the lines of text blurring into one. Matt's message flashed up in the corner, a lifeline in the digital sea.

"Got everything?" his words read, simple, to the point.

"Everything and more," I typed back. "It's a mess, Matt."

"Any leads?"

"So apparently, the latest new evidence is a witness statement from Carol, the neighbor, saying that she saw Will push Angela down the stairs. She had been out that night with some friends and was on her way home when she saw light inside the Jennings' house; startled at this, she looked in through the window, and that's when she saw it. She saw Will at the top of the stairs, arguing with Angela and then angrily pushing her down the stairs. Apparently, details in her statement fit with forensic findings at the scene, like that she grabbed the railing to steady herself and then received another push before she fell. The forensic files say that there are definitely signs of someone gripping the railing, like smeared fingerprints. Carol says in the statement that she didn't want to tell anyone back then, as she feared for her own life, but also because she liked Will and didn't want him to go to jail. But as the years went by, she couldn't keep it inside. I think something is off with this statement. Carol's hiding something, but I never got around to asking her about it when I saw her," I replied. My fingers hovered over the keys, hesitation a rare weight. "Will's innocent. I know it."

"Trust your gut, Eva Rae. You're the best at this."

"I'm not so sure anymore. Time's running out." I glanced at the clock. "Trial's in two days."

"Damn." The pause in our conversation stretched out, tense and electric. "You've got this, Rae."

"Thanks, Miller." But even as I sent the message, doubt gnawed at me. Two days. Forty-eight hours to dismantle lies wrapped tight around an innocent man's future.

I snapped the laptop shut, urgency clawing at my insides. Evidence didn't lie—but people did—time to pick apart the truth from the carefully constructed facades.

Two days. The deadline was a drumbeat in my head, quickening with every passing second.

Chapter 15

THEN:

Angela perched on the edge of the couch, her fingers entwined in a tight weave. The silence of the room pressed against her like an unwelcome guest, amplifying the drumbeat of her heart. She eyed her phone, its black screen a gateway to potential solace or further doubt.

A deep breath. She reached out, the device cold and slick in her clammy grip. Her thumb hovered, then descended with purpose, pressing the familiar number. The dial tone hummed.

"Sam," she whispered when the line clicked alive.

"Angela?" The name came sharp, tinged with concern. Hearing her best friend's voice made it hard for Angela not to burst into tears. She and Samantha had known each other since elementary school.

"What's wrong? You sound troubled?"

"It's Will." Her voice quivered, betraying the façade of calm she was trying so desperately to uphold. "Something's... off. I can't shake this feeling. I might be going crazy, but I just think that something is going on with him. Tell me I'm not crazy."

"Talk to me." Sam's command cut through the static. "Explain it all to me. What's going on?"

"He stays at work late at night and comes up with strange excuses when I ask about receipts I find in his pants pockets when doing laundry that are from restaurants or coffee houses. It's nothing, he says. Just work dinners and meetings. He's a pediatrician. Who is he meeting with? He won't tell. I hear him whisper on the phone or hang up suddenly when I enter a room. He's hiding something; I know it. I can't stand it anymore."

Angela's words tumbled out, a cascade of fear and uncertainty.

"That doesn't sound good, Angela." Sam's tone sharpened, focused as a laser. "And you're sure you're not just in your head, seeing things?"

"No, he's always heading to meetings or going on trips out of town, and he suddenly changed his password for his computer. I guessed the new one, though, as it was our daughter's birthday, but still. Who does that? If they have nothing to hide?" Angela's breaths came rapid, punctuating each revelation. "I'm not imagining things. That's what Will says every time I try to bring it up. Stop saying that. It makes me feel like there's something wrong with me."

"Okay, okay, I hear you. Now, I want you to remain calm for now, and we'll figure this out. You're not alone in this," Sam assured, her voice a lifeline in the tumultuous sea of Angela's worries.

"Thanks, Sam." Angela's grip on the phone loosened, a fragile relief blooming within her chest.

"But Angie, sweetie, you can't let this eat at you. You deserve to know the truth." Sam's voice resonated with an unwavering certainty that seemed to pierce the fog of Angela's trepidation. "To know you're not being crazy, seeing things that aren't there. You need to do something."

"Action, huh?" Angela's words were half-question, half-whisper, as if speaking them louder might make them too real.

"Remember when we were kids? We never let anyone push us around. Not then, not now," Sam recalled, a touch of nostalgia lending warmth to her steady cadence.

A smile tugged at the corner of Angela's mouth. Childhood memories flickered—a shared resilience, a bond unbroken through decades. "You're right," she affirmed, strength creeping into her voice.

"Good. Now, go find out what he's hiding. Do whatever it takes. Go on his computer and go through all his social media accounts. Check for dating sites or other sites where he might be talking to other women. And then, at some point, you have to go on his phone and check that. When he is sleeping, perhaps. You gotta do some work here. Everyone leaves traces in the digital world of cheating. That's where you need to look. No one can hide their affairs online. And keep me updated."

"Okay."

With a click, the line went dead. Silence enveloped the room once more, but Angela no longer felt its oppressive weight. She rose, a sentinel in her own life, eyes narrowing with purpose. The living room stretched before her, each step deliberate as she crossed the expanse of soft carpet.

Angela's shadow stretched before her as she approached the study, a silent harbinger of the storm brewing within. She paused at the threshold, hand on the cold doorknob, gathering the shards of her resolve. With a soft click, the door yielded to her touch and swung open.

The room was still, dust motes dancing in the slanting

light through half-drawn blinds. She stepped inside, every sense heightened, scanning for disruptions in the familiar landscape of Will's private sanctum. There it was—the desk, a tableau of chaos amidst the order, strewn with papers, pens, and the silver gleam of his computer.

She approached, a quiet gasp escaping her lips as her fingertips grazed the leather-bound surface of his chair—his throne of secrets. Her heart thrummed against her ribs, urging her on. Angela leaned forward, her breath catching in her throat as she sifted through the topmost papers.

"Receipts, bills... nothing," she whispered, each word punctuated by the rustle of paper.

Her hands, though trembling, were methodical in their quest, betraying none of the gentleness that usually graced her touch. Each document told a story, but not the one she needed to hear. She rifled through them faster now, searching for a telltale sign—a name, a number, anything.

"Come on, Will, where is it?" The words were a hiss of frustration, her patience waning with each fruitless turn of the page. Her fingers found an envelope, unmarked and sealed. A flicker of hope surged, her pulse quickening as she carefully opened the flap, revealing...

"Utilities," she muttered, discarding it with a flutter of disappointment.

Angela pressed on, driven by the gnawing uncertainty that had lodged itself in her mind. She could feel Sam's encouragement like a distant echo, spurring her onward. The last of the pile offered no revelation, just the mundane detritus of daily life.

"Nothing," she breathed, a tremor in her voice belying her outward composure. But she wasn't done—not yet. The computer sat there, a silent witness, waiting to yield its digital secrets. She had been on it many times now, but she had never looked at his social media. Now, it was time.

Angela's hand hovered above it, a momentary hesitation before her resolve crystallized into action.

"Time to dig deeper," she affirmed, a newfound edge to her tone, ready to peel back the layers of Will's virtual world.

Angela hunched over the computer, a glint of determination in her bright blue eyes. She clicked it open, its screen illuminating the dim room with a pale glow. Her fingers hovered, then dove to the keys, typing with an urgency that betrayed her composed exterior. The familiar hum of the machine came alive as she navigated past the desktop, straight to the core of Will's online footsteps—the internet browser.

"History," she whispered, her voice steady but laced with a hint of desperation. She found the tab and clicked it.

Nothing.

A blank slate stared back at her; the history had been cleared once again—a digital void where secrets should have been. Angela's heart sank, then pounded with renewed vigor against her ribcage.

"Okay, what are you hiding?" Her tone was sharp, slicing through the silence of the study.

She moved on to social media, clicking through accounts with swift precision. Photos, messages, timelines —all mundane, all painfully ordinary. She found no secret accounts under different names, nor any strange messages in his DMs. He didn't have a dating profile on Facebook, so it wasn't there either. Emails next; her fingers danced across the keys, summoning his inbox to her scrutiny. Promotions, newsletters, work correspondence—every subject line a dead end.

"Damn it, Will." The words were a mere breath, frustration seeping into her resolve like a cold draft.

DARK LITTLE SERETCS

Angela sat back, the laptop's soft glow casting shadows across her face. She closed her eyes for a moment, collecting herself, before leaning in once more. A deep breath, and she returned to the hunt, unwilling to let the trail go cold.

Angela's jaw clenched, a physical manifestation of the frustration boiling within her. She refused to succumb to defeat. Inhaling deeply, she steadied her trembling hands and focused on the task at hand. With a click, she summoned the file explorer, its window opening like the entrance to a labyrinth.

"Come on," she muttered under her breath.

Her gaze was sharp, dissecting the screen for any anomaly, any clue that might pierce the shroud of secrecy. Folders named with meticulous banality flashed before her: "Work Documents," "Tax Returns," "Family Photos." Nothing screamed deception; nothing whispered betrayal.

"Nothing," she exhaled, each click a step further into the abyss of the ordinary.

"Hidden files…." The words were a lifeline, an idea to grasp in a sea of digital normalcy. Her fingers danced across the keyboard, commands flowing from her mind to reveal what might lie beneath the surface. Settings adjusted, options changed—she peeled back the layers of the digital facade.

"Where are you?" The intensity of her scrutiny did not waver as folder after folder opened to reveal their contents. "Vacation Plans" held itineraries and hotel bookings, "Recipes" a collection of culinary aspirations never realized.

"Insurance Policies," "Car Maintenance" —each label a beacon of mundane responsibility. Her anticipation, once a flame, flickered in the draught of disappointment. She dove deeper, hoping for a spark, a sign.

"Nothing," she repeated, the word a bitter taste in her mouth. She sank back and returned to the physical world, desperate to find something... anything. She opened the drawers one after the other, frantically searching for a clue, when her hand felt something. A secret compartment? She pulled it open and looked inside. She felt her blood freeze.

What the heck is this, Will?

That's when she heard the front door slam shut and Will's footsteps enter. She stared at what she had found, then heard him call her name.

"Angela? Where are you?"

Quickly, she put the object in her pocket, then snuck out of the room, closing the door behind her.

"Angela?" she heard him call again. "Where are you, honey?"

She pressed away her tears with all the power she had, then forced a smile.

"Up here, Will. Be right down."

Chapter 16

The phone rang, jarring me out of my thoughts. I picked up, my heart pounding.

"Eva Rae Thomas." My voice sounded shaky.

"Agent Thomas? Or is it detective? I don't know all the titles and formalities. This is Samantha, I'm Angela's childhood friend. I spoke to Diane, and she told me to contact you. I have information about Angela and her husband, Will, that I think might be useful. Can you meet me at the Coffee House on St. George's Street?"

Adrenaline shot through me. Something, finally. I was desperate for anything at this point.

"I'll be right there."

The café was nearly empty at this hour. I spotted Samantha in a corner booth, fidgeting with her coffee mug. Her eyes widened when she saw me approach.

"Thank you for meeting me." I slid into the seat across from her. "It means a lot to me."

I ordered a coffee, and the waitress left. "So, what's going on? What can you tell me?"

Samantha glanced around furtively before leaning in.

"Like six months before her death, Angela called me… frantic."

"Frantic? Why was she frantic?" I asked as the server brought me my coffee. It was very strong. I poured in some sugar and swirled the spoon.

"She was certain that Will was having an affair," she said. "But she couldn't find any evidence, not on his computer, social media, or phone, and it was driving her crazy. He showed all the symptoms of a cheating husband, being distant, staying late at work, hushed conversations over the phone, and so on."

"Did she ever find any evidence of this affair?" I asked, sipping my steaming hot coffee.

"No, but she found something else. Something that explained everything. Especially why he was so distant."

My eyes grew wide. This was news.

"What did she find?"

"She said she'd been looking for evidence of his affair in his home office and found a bag of pills in a drawer. Oxycodone."

My mind raced, putting the pieces together. Oxycodone—a powerful, addictive painkiller. "That would certainly explain his odd behavior. Did she confront Will about it?"

Samantha nodded. "He confessed he'd been battling an addiction for the past two years. Angela was devastated. She didn't know what to do."

I scribbled furiously in my notebook. This changed everything. If Angela knew about Will's addiction, did she use that knowledge against him somehow? He was a doctor and wouldn't be able to work if it was found out. Or did Will's increasingly erratic behavior put her in danger?

It painted a different picture of the oh-so-perfect

couple I had entertained until now. It didn't exactly exonerate Will. But if I was to find the truth, I needed to get down to all the ugly parts, too, and this was definitely one.

I met Samantha's gaze. "Thank you for telling me this. This is very useful information indeed. If you think of anything else…."

"I'll call you." She stood abruptly, grabbing her purse. "I have to go. I have to get to work. Please find out what really happened to Angela. She was my best friend. I loved her dearly."

"I will. I promise."

As I watched Samantha hurry out of the café, a plan began forming in my mind. I needed to search Angela and Will's house for any evidence of the addiction. It wouldn't acquit Will from the murder case, but it was a piece of the puzzle, and experience had taught me that all pieces were necessary to get the complete picture.

Chapter 17

I left the cafe, my mind reeling with the new information. The Florida sun beat down on me as I walked to my car, but I hardly noticed the heat. All I could think about was getting to Angela and Will's house and finding that evidence.

As I drove, Alex called me, and I picked up. "Hey, buddy. What's up?"

"What are you doing, Mom? When are you coming home?"

I sighed, guilt nagging at me again. "In a few days. I promise."

"Don't forget my game on Saturday, Mommy."

"I won't. I'll be there, buddy. I promise."

I ended the call, feeling worse than ever. I hated being away from my family, but I knew I couldn't rest until I found the truth.

Minutes later, I pulled up to Angela and Will's house. The place looked almost eerie in its emptiness. I took a deep breath and got out of the car, my hand instinctively resting on my holster.

The front door was locked, but I found a way in through the sliding door in the back that was left unlocked. As I stepped inside, the silence engulfed me. Being here felt wrong.

I made my way to the home office, my heart pounding. If there were evidence of Will's addiction anywhere, it would be here. I started with the desk drawers, rifling through papers and files. Nothing.

Then I remembered Samantha's words. The pills had been in a drawer. I crouched down, pulling open the bottom drawer. It was empty, save for a few old magazines. I was about to close it when something caught my eye.

A small, almost imperceptible gap in the wood at the back of the drawer. My pulse quickened as I felt along the edge, my fingers searching for a latch or a button. There. The false bottom popped open with a soft click, revealing a small, hidden compartment.

And inside was a plastic baggie filled with white pills. Jackpot.

I pulled out the baggie, my hands shaking slightly. This was it. The evidence that would prove Samantha's story. It showed things were bad between them, yes. But what did it mean? How did it play into her death?

Did Angela take any of the pills, and that's why she lost her balance and fell? Was she addicted, too?

I shook my head, pushing the thought aside. I needed to focus on the facts. I slipped the baggie into an evidence bag and continued my search, moving from room to room with a renewed sense of purpose.

In the kitchen, I methodically opened each drawer, not really expecting to find anything. But in the third drawer, tucked beneath a stack of takeout menus, I found something that made my heart skip a beat.

A small, leather-bound notebook.

With trembling fingers, I opened it to the first page. Angela's neat handwriting filled the paper, dated just four months before her death.

"I found the pills again today. I don't know what to do. I'm scared for Will, for our family. I tried to talk to him, but he just got angry. He says he needs them—that they help him cope with the stress of work. But I know they're changing him. He's not the man I married anymore."

I flipped through the pages, and each entry was more disturbing than the last.

"He's getting worse. The mood swings, the outbursts. I'm afraid he'll hurt himself or, worse, someone else. I have to do something. I have to save him from himself."

The final entry was dated a month before Angela's death.

"I can't take it anymore. I'm going to confront him tonight. I'm going to give him a choice. Either it's the pills or us. If he doesn't stop, I'm taking the kids and leaving. I won't let his addiction destroy our family. I just pray he makes the right choice."

I closed the notebook, my heart heavy with the weight of Angela's words. She had been trying to help him, to save their family. And now she was gone.

I slipped the notebook into my bag, along with the pills. I had what I needed. It was time to put the pieces together and find out what happened that night. If I was being honest, it didn't look good for Will.

As I walked out of the house, I couldn't shake the feeling that there was more to this story than meets the eye. Angela's notebook had opened up a whole new line of questioning.

I got in my car and sat for a moment, my mind racing. I needed to talk to Will and confront him with this new evidence. But first, I had to make a phone call.

I dialed the number of my trusted medical expert, Dr. Sampson. If anyone could shed light on the effects of those pills, it was him.

As the phone rang, I stared out the window at the empty house, a silent witness to the tragedy that had unfolded within its walls. I just hoped I would find the truth somewhere amidst the secrets and lies. For Angela's sake and the sake of her family, I had to.

Chapter 18

Carol's fingers fumbled with the tie of her robe, the knot stubborn and tight. She tugged it loose, letting the sash fall to her sides. She brushed through her graying brown hair and stifled a yawn—all her nightly rituals, but tonight, they were interrupted by the faintest scrape, a whisper of sound from the floor below.

Carol didn't feel safe. All day, she felt like someone was watching her every move, and now, all alone in her house, it had become worse.

She stilled, breath held, the silence that followed thick with the weight of unspoken fears. The house seemed to hold its breath with her. Carol strained her ears, seeking the comfort of a rational explanation—a branch against the window, the house settling—but nothing came.

She didn't believe it.

"It's probably nothing," she murmured, the words swallowed by the quiet around her. Yet her heart betrayed her calm, thrumming a warning against her ribs.

Chewing on her bottom lip, a nervous habit she could never shake, Carol edged to the stairway. Each step was a silent plea: don't creak; don't give me away. Her nightgown whispered against her legs as she walked, ghost-like in the moonlit darkness.

"Hello?"

Her voice was louder than intended. It darted into the shadows, searching for an intruder who might lurk there. But only silence greeted her, a void that mocked her with its emptiness.

"Is someone there?"

Her hand reached for the wall, fingertips grazing the cool surface for balance. The question felt foolish the moment it left her lips—why announce herself? Why not flip a light switch and reveal all? But fear clouded judgment, and her actions ran on instinct, the primal part of her brain screaming danger even as logic whispered calm.

The tension twisted tighter with each unanswered call, a coiled spring ready to burst. Alone in the dark, Carol could almost hear her own heartbeat, loud in the stillness that followed. The scent of dust and old wood filled her nostrils, familiar yet suddenly foreign as she stood at the top of the stairs, a sentinel in her own home, shrouded in uncertainty and the pressing sense of something amiss.

Fingers trembling, Carol descended, each step down the staircase a mounting dread. She willed her legs to move, the air thick with the sound of her ragged breaths. She reached the bottom, every shadow a specter in the dim glow of the hallway nightlight.

"Hello?" she tried again.

Still, only silence met her. She flipped the light switch, and the living room came to light. It looked the same as always. She walked to the front door and checked that it was locked. It was—no sign of anyone having tried to enter. The windows were the same. She pulled the curtains, feeling a chill run down her spine as she felt eyes on her. She turned with a gasp, but no one was there.

"Enough of this nonsense," she told herself, looking at the clock. It was late. She had an early morning and should be in bed by now. She walked to the light switch and threw a glance around the living room and kitchen area, then decided it was time to let it go. She turned off the lights, then walked up the stairs with faster, more determined steps.

This was silly. Really.

The bedroom door creaked shut behind her after she entered, a feeble barrier between her and the unknown. Her hand lingered on the knob for longer than necessary. Safety was an illusion; she knew it as her gaze swept across the comfort of rumpled sheets and framed photos.

A floorboard groaned next to her.

Carol's blood ran cold. She spun, her heart leaping to her throat. A figure—dark and indistinct—loomed where, seconds ago, there had been nothing but air. How? The window—it was open. She never locked it up here.

Lunging forward, the shape shattered the stillness. No time for screams, no breath for pleas. Fear rooted her to the carpet as instinct screamed: Move!

Clawing at reality, Carol's mind raced. The intruder advanced, relentless. This was survival, raw and unfiltered.

Carol's fist connected with a dull thud against the attacker's torso, her knuckles screaming in protest. She recoiled, breath ragged, and lashed out again—with the heel of her palm this time—aiming for the shadowy visage that twisted away with maddening agility.

"Get away from me!"

Her voice was a sharp crack in the thick silence, more to steel her resolve than to intimidate. The room reeled as

DARK LITTLE SERETCS

she pivoted on one foot, and then she kicked, her leg slicing the air and hitting the intruder's leg.

A heavy shove sent her stumbling back; her spine jarred against the edge of the dresser. Trinkets clattered, cascading to the floor in a rain of memories and glass. The lamp wobbled perilously at the commotion, its bulb casting erratic shadows as it, too, succumbed to gravity's call.

"Stay away from me!" Carol's shout was punctuated by another wild blow, her athletic frame coiling and uncoiling like a spring, each movement fueled by primal terror and the will to survive.

The attacker surged forward, arms flailing, their bulk a weapon in itself. Carol ducked, a picture frame grazing her hair and shattering against the wall. She felt the sting of splinters and the warmth of a trickle that might have been sweat or blood.

In the chaos, a chair toppled, the sound deafening as it hit the ground. Fabric tore. Metal screeched. Her assailant stumbled, momentarily thrown off balance by the upturned furniture.

"Help!" she screamed, though she knew it would not come. Carol seized the moment, her body a blur of motion as she drove her knee upward, connecting with something solid. A grunt, not hers, filled the room—a small victory swallowed by the struggle.

She couldn't let up, every cell in her body screaming in defiance. This was her space, her sanctuary, now defiled by violence. She would not yield. Each breath was fire in her chest, each heartbeat a drum rallying her to fight.

"Stop—"

The word was cut short as they grappled. Fingers found hair and yanked cruelly. Carol twisted, biting back a cry, her elbow flying back with all the force desperation could muster. She hit him. It was a satisfying impact, followed by a curse that sounded barely human.

Her world narrowed to the melee, the visceral dance of attack and defense. Adrenaline sharpened her senses, every thud, every gasp etched into the fabric of the night. The room bore witness, silent but for the cacophony of destruction they wrought upon it.

"Get away from me!" It was a plea, a demand, a battle cry. She wouldn't go quietly or be extinguished without leaving her mark or fighting tooth and nail for every second that pulsed through her veins.

Carol's knuckles ached, and her arms felt heavy as lead. A vicious swipe from the attacker sent her stumbling backward, her pulse thundering in her ears. Weak light glinted off the edge of the nightstand, where the silhouette of a lamp promised a fleeting chance at defense.

"Get away!"

Her voice was a razor slicing through the thick air. She lunged, fingers grazing the ceramic base, her grip slipping but just holding.

The assailant surged forward, a mass of dark intent. Carol swung the lamp like a club, its arc short-lived. The figure's hand snatched it mid-flight, wrenching it away with brute force. It happened too fast—her only weapon was now in their control.

"Please—"

The plea evaporated as pain exploded across her temple. White-hot, searing. A crash resonated as her legs buckled, her body no longer hers to command.

Silence descended, a suffocating blanket. Only the ragged rhythm of Carol's breath pierced the stillness, each inhale a shard of glass in her lungs.

Vision fractured, a kaleidoscope of shadows and light, Carol's mind clawed at consciousness. The floor was cold against her cheek, the texture of the carpet pressing into her skin, offering an anchor in the spinning world. She dragged her body forward, inch by laborious inch, her fingers grappling with the plush pile, seeking leverage, anything to propel her toward safety.

"Help," she gasped, the word a mere whisper, dissipating before it could reach beyond the confines of the room. Her hand flailed, searching for her phone, for a lifeline. It wasn't there—had it been on the nightstand? Had it been knocked away in the struggle?

Her attacker's breaths were harsh, ragged storms that filled the space between them. Carol didn't dare look back; she couldn't afford to lose the precious focus required to inch away from the looming presence.

Darkness crept along the edges of her sight, a creeping tide ready to engulf her. Panic spiked, a fresh surge of adrenaline, but her body betrayed her, sluggish, movements disjointed as if she were submerged in water.

"Please," she tried again, the plea strangled, caught in the throes of encroaching oblivion. Her arm buckled, no longer able to sustain her weight. She felt herself slipping, the room tilting on its axis, the last vestiges of hope flickering out.

This is it, a thought floated up through the fog, detached, observing the end as it unfolded. Her fate, once written in the stars, was now rewritten in violence and shadow.

The darkness welcomed her, an inevitable embrace as the figure above moved closer, their intent clear, final.

Carol's chest rose and fell, slower now, each breath a shallow echo. Silence clawed its way into the room, thick and heavy, settling over the chaos of upturned furniture and scattered belongings.

A final shudder ran through her, muscles going slack.

The world narrowed to a point, a single frame of stillness in which she lay surrendered to the inevitable.

Her eyelids fluttered, a last feeble protest before they stilled, the haunted fear that lived in her eyes giving way to emptiness. The air itself seemed to pause, the fabric of the night holding its breath.

The attacker stood motionless, watching as life slipped from Carol's grasp. There was no triumph in their stance, only the quiet certainty of a purpose fulfilled.

On the floor, Carol lay defeated, with the struggle imprinted on the disarray around her. Her once vibrant spirit was now just a fading wisp mingling with the shadows.

No words were spoken. There was no need for them when the silence spoke volumes, a chilling testament to the void left behind. The question lingered, unasked but palpable:

Why?

Chapter 19

I jolted up in my seat, the screams tearing into the silence of the night—a piercing, frantic sound that set my pulse hammering. Instinct took over. I had been working, going over evidence and the case files repeatedly, without being able to get to the bottom of this case, so I decided to go for a drive. To clear my thoughts. Without even knowing it, I ended up in front of Will and Angela's house, wondering about their story. And that's when I heard it.

The screams didn't let up—desperate, chilling. Every second counted.

I snatched my badge from the passenger seat, put it around my neck, and opened the car's front door. The Florida air slapped me awake. I sprinted across the dew-damp grass, my gun firm in my grip, ready for whatever hell awaited.

My heart hammered against my ribs, each beat a drumroll urging me faster. The soles of my feet slapped the pavement, and my breath came in ragged gasps as I raced toward the house. Adrenaline surged, turning my blood to fire, honing every sense to a razor's edge. The night air was a humid whip against my skin, but inside, I burned with a single purpose—to stop whatever horror those screams had promised.

"Carol!" I shouted, reaching the front door and hammering my fist into it.

No answer, only the echo of my own voice against the silent facade of the house. "It's Agent Thomas! Open up!"

Still nothing. Panic clawed at my gut, the silence more terrifying than the screams that had ceased.

Without hesitation, I repositioned my weight and drove my foot into the door, just beside the handle. The frame splintered with a satisfying crack, and the door flew open under the force of my kick. Gun raised, senses on high alert, I crossed the threshold. The darkness of the house loomed before me, a gaping maw hiding untold terrors, and I stepped into its depths.

The stillness was a void that my heartbeat shattered. Upstairs, I found her in the bedroom. Carol Rudolph, a crumpled heap of life unlived, sprawled across the bedroom floor. Blood—a stark, crimson halo—seeped into the white carpet, staining it with finality. Her eyes stared at nothingness, a silent scream etched onto her face. A blunt object, a lamp, its purpose twisted to violence, lay discarded nearby, smeared with the evidence of brutality.

"God," I choked out, bile rising. The room spun, and every nerve ending within me recoiled, but I steadied myself. This was no time to falter. I noticed the window was open. That wasn't a common sight in Florida, where you always strived to keep the heat out. I ran to look down and saw the ladder discarded in the grass below. The killer was gone.

I yanked my phone from my pocket, fingers trembling as I dialed 911.

"This is Eva Rae Thomas, FBI. I need units at 166 Hawthorne Road immediately. We have a homicide." My usually steady voice betrayed a tremor of urgency, threading through each syllable like a live wire.

"Please, hurry," I added, almost whispering as if volume could beckon speed. "She's gone."

The wail of sirens crescendoed as red and blue lights strobed through the windows. I stepped back from Carol's lifeless form, my mind whirring with the cold machinery of protocol and procedure. Within minutes, the house swarmed with uniforms, their grim faces a mirror to my own dread.

He arrived like a shadow cast by a looming storm cloud: Detective Larson. The air seemed to bristle as he stepped into the room, his gaze locking onto me with a familiarity that spelled trouble. Larson was broad-shouldered, his jaw set in a way that suggested smiles were a rarity. His eyes, sharp and calculating, had always regarded me with suspicion, even before tonight's grim discovery.

"Thomas," he grunted, barely a greeting but loaded with disdain.

"Larson," I acknowledged, keeping my voice neutral despite the heat rising in my chest.

"Let's take a walk," he said, gesturing with a tilt of his head toward the door. It wasn't a request.

I followed him outside, the night air doing little to cool the tension between us. We reached his cruiser, its doors yawning open like a trap. He gestured again, this time more pointedly. "Get in."

There was no use in arguing.

The ride to the station was a silent duel of wills. My fingers itched for something to do, a report to fill out, anything to distract from the weight of Larson's glare in the rearview mirror.

We arrived, and the sterile light of the interrogation room welcomed me with a harsh buzz. Larson slid a recorder across the table, the click of its button punctuating the beginning of a long night.

"State your name for the record."

"Eva Rae Thomas."

"Agent Thomas, tell me why you were at the victim's house tonight."

"I heard screams, and I went to help."

"Armed and ready to kick down doors? That's quite the neighborhood watch program you're running. What were you doing in that neighborhood?"

"I couldn't sleep."

"And went for a drive in that particular neighborhood? Quite the coincidence, don't you think? On the very night of a murder?" His words jabbed at me like accusations made steel.

"I was looking at the Jennings' house."

"Kind of an odd hour to do that. Where were you before the screams?"

"In my car."

"Anyone to corroborate that?"

"Are you seriously suggesting—?"

"Answer the question, Thomas."

"Of course not. I was alone."

"Right," he sneered, as if my answer left a bad taste. "And tell me again, why were you in Carol Rudolph's house?"

I sighed, annoyed at this. "I heard screams, Detective. I ran there to help. I protect people. Or at least, I try to."

"Try and fail, apparently." His tone was a mix of mockery and challenge.

"Enough, Larson. You have zero reason to hold me."

"Except for being the only suspect in a murder case."

"Because I reported it?"

"Because you found the body. Because you have no alibi. Because—"

"Because you've never liked me. Is that it? Personal vendettas now count as evidence?"

He leaned forward, hands flat on the table. "This isn't personal, Thomas. This is about justice."

"Then find the real killer instead of wasting time with me."

"Trust me, I intend to."

Larson stood up abruptly, his chair scraping against the floor like an echo of his frustration.

"You're free to go… for now. But don't leave town. We're not finished here."

"Wouldn't dream of it," I retorted, pushing back from the table, my resolve hardening like armor. "And when you're done chasing shadows, I'll be finding the truth."

I walked out of that interrogation room, a mixture of indignation and adrenaline fueling each step. Larson might have doubted me, but I knew one thing for certain: a killer was loose, and we had been looking in all the wrong places. The answer I needed to find now was why. Why did Carol have to die? I was determined that if we found that out, we would know who our killer was.

The doors of the police station swung shut behind me, the echo of their finality sending a chill down my spine. Dawn was breaking, painting the sky in strokes of pink and orange, but its beauty was lost on me. I took a ragged breath, the taste of freedom bittersweet on my tongue.

I was out, yet not cleared; liberated, yet shackled by suspicion. The detective's eyes still burned into my back, his doubt a shadow that clung as tightly as the salty breeze of Cocoa Beach. I touched my badge, feeling its outline—a reminder of who I was and what I needed to do.

As I Ubered back to my car, I kept thinking of Carol. Her lifeless body flashed before my eyes, haunting and urging me to act. My fingers itched for the comfort of my gun, for the sense of control it gave when everything else was slipping through my grasp like sand.

Once back in the neighborhood, I slid behind the wheel, the leather seat cold against my weary body. Every bone in me screamed for sleep, for escape from the night's relentless questioning. But slumber was a siren's song—tempting, yet dangerous.

The key turned, the engine roared to life, and with it, so did my resolve. The detective be damned; his narrow suspicions wouldn't deter me. There was a killer out there, a predator masking in plain sight, and I would not rest until I had unmasked them. I grabbed my phone.

"Diane, we need to talk," I said. "Meet me at the Coffee House on St. George's Street in an hour."

I hung up, determined as ever. As I pulled away from the curb, the sun crested the horizon, its rays like fingers peeling back the darkness. A new day, a fresh start.

"Carol, I will find who did this to you," I promised the silent dawn. "And they will pay." My grip tightened on the steering wheel. No more running, no more hiding.

The real killer was about to meet their match.

Chapter 20

THEN:

Angela's fingers trailed along Will's arm, her touch light but insistent. She nestled closer, her breath warm against his neck. Once, twice, she pressed her lips to his skin, a silent plea.

Will's response was a quiet, "Not tonight, Angie."

"Come on, Will," Angela's voice held an edge, a whine that grated more with each syllable. She shifted, the sheets whispering with her movement, her knee nudging his leg. He turned away, a wall of flesh between them.

"Seriously?" Her tone spiked, disbelief and something else—resentment—coloring it ugly.

"Angie, please." His words were a tired exhale, his body tense beside her in the same bed where they had once made two beautiful children but hadn't made love since.

"You don't want me?" The question was a sharp blade, pointed and accusatory.

"Angela, stop." Will's refusal was firmer now, his patience fraying at the edges.

Her hand snapped back as if bitten. Eyes narrowing, she propped herself up on an elbow, the softness in her face giving way to hard lines.

"Is there someone else, Will?"

"Oh, my God. Are we back to that again? Of course not." His answer came too quickly, defensive.

"Then why?" she demanded, her voice climbing, the question like a gunshot in the quiet room. "Why won't you be with me?"

"Angie, I'm just not…."

Will's voice trailed off, his struggle palpable in the dim light.

"Not what? Interested? Aroused?" Angela's mocking tone sliced through the air, her jealousy a living thing between them.

"Stop it." Will's protest was weak, his resistance crumbling.

"Or maybe," Angela continued relentlessly, "you're getting it elsewhere."

"Angela, that's enough!" Will's outburst filled the room, a brief flare of anger in the growing storm.

Will bolted upright, the mattress recoiling from his sudden movement. He swung his legs out of bed, standing in one fluid motion.

"I'm not in the mood, Angela," he snapped, a growl underpinning his words. "That's all it is. Don't make it into something it's not."

"You're never in the mood!" Angela shot back, sitting up, her hair a disheveled halo around her head. "What is it then? You find me repulsive?"

"Christ, no," he said, pacing at the foot of the bed, his hands raking through his hair. "I've told you about the meds—the pills I've been taking and how they screw with everything."

"Medication." She spat the word as if it tasted foul on her tongue. "That's your excuse? Convenient."

"Excuse?" Will stopped pacing and faced her. "It's not an excuse—it's the damn truth!"

"Or maybe," she pressed, her voice dripping with venom, "it's just a cover for all your little escapades." Her eyes were cold and piercing.

"Escapades?" He echoed the accusation with disbelief. "You think I have the energy for that?"

"Energy or not," she hurled back, "you're lying to me. There's someone else, isn't there? I can tell."

"Angela," Will pleaded, his voice strained, "You know my situation. Why would I lie about this?"

"Because you're a man, Will!" she hissed, her blue eyes flashing dangerously. "And I've seen how women look at you—the way they linger. I'm not blind. Especially that bitch next door."

"Your jealousy…." Will's voice trailed off, his anger subsiding into resignation. "It's blinding you."

Will's shadow loomed against the soft glow of the bedside lamp, his silhouette jagged with tension.

"You want the truth?" His voice cut through the silence, sharp and raw.

"Of course I do!" Angela's reply was a whip-crack in the stillness, her figure stiff as she clutched the sheets to her chest.

"Fine." Will's breath came out in a harsh exhale. "I can't perform, okay? I can't get it up." The words tumbled from him like boulders, heavy with shame. "Because of the pills I've been taking."

Angela froze, her hands gripping the fabric so tight her knuckles turned white. Silence stretched between them, thick and suffocating.

"Happy now?" Will's face twisted in a grimace, his vulnerability laid bare beneath the scrutiny of her gaze.

Her lips parted, but no sound emerged. She could only stare, taking in the confession that hung in the air, palpable and shattering. It didn't last long. Angela's skepticism was a blade, her disbelief a sharp edge against Will's exposed truth.

"You really expect me to believe that?" Her voice was ice, her posture rigid against the headboard.

"Angela—"

"Save it, Will." The mockery seeped from her words, thick and venomous. "I've heard enough of your excuses."

"Excuses?" His eyes darkened, the hurt evident. "You think I'm lying about this?"

"Wouldn't be the first time," she spat.

The room seemed to shrink with the intensity of her accusation, walls closing in on him, trapping him.

"Damn it, Angela!" His fist hit the mattress, frustration booming. "Why can't you just trust me?"

"Trust?" She laughed, a sound devoid of humor. "That's rich, coming from you."

"Stop it!" His voice rose, the plea dissolving into anger.

"Make me!" She challenged, her eyes sparking fire.

"Is that what you want?" He threw his hands up, the gesture one of defeat. "To push me until I break?"

"Maybe I do." Her tone was lethal, each word a calculated strike. "Maybe then you'll stop lying through your teeth."

"God, you're impossible!" Will shot back, the last of his restraint snapping.

"Right, because I'm the problem here." She sneered, leaning forward, her face twisted with scorn. "Not the impotent husband who can't satisfy his wife because he sleeps around."

DARK LITTLE SERETCS

"Enough, Angela!" He moved away, the space between them charged with unspoken wounds.

"Where are you going?" Her challenge followed him as he paced the room, a caged animal seeking escape.

"Anywhere but here," he muttered, running a hand through his hair in exasperation.

"Run away, then!" She taunted. "Like you always do!"

"Running is better than this insanity." His retort was a low growl, the sound of a cornered man.

"Admit it. You're cheating." Her accusation was a dagger aimed at his heart.

"Believe what you want." His shoulders slumped, surrendering to the impossibility of reason.

"Believing lies is your specialty, not mine." Her words were final, sealing the chasm between them.

Angela's hand shot out, seizing the glass vase from the nightstand with manic energy. It hurtled through the air, missing Will by mere inches as it shattered against the wall. Fragments cascaded down like glittering rain.

"Damn it, Angela!" Will sidestepped another incoming missile—a book this time—its pages fluttering helplessly to the floor.

"Look at you," she spat, her voice seething with contempt as she grabbed the next available object, a framed photograph. "So pathetic, pretending it's the drugs."

"Angela, stop!" He lunged, trying to intercept her flailing arms.

"Stop?" She laughed, a hollow sound devoid of any true humor. "Why? Because you can't handle the truth?"

"This isn't you." His plea was earnest, eyes searching for the woman he knew beneath the fury.

"Isn't me?" She threw the picture, the glass cracking on

impact. "Or is it just not the docile wife you want me to be?"

"Please." He caught her wrist mid-swing, halting another throw. "I'm telling you the truth."

"Truth?" Her lip curled. "Your truth is a lie!"

"Angela." He held her gaze, his own filled with pain. "The drugs—they've killed my desire. I'm not cheating on you."

"Lies!" She writhed against his grip, but he held fast.

"Believe me." His voice cracked, the rawness betraying his inner turmoil.

"Believe a cheater?" She wrenched free, panting, her energy finally waning.

"Angela…." His shoulders drooped, a silent plea for understanding etched in his posture.

"Sleep wherever you want, with whoever you want," she hissed, the fight draining from her as quickly as it had erupted. "Just not with me."

He watched, heart leaden, as she stormed out of the bedroom, the door slamming shut with a finality that echoed through the hollow silence.

Angela collapsed onto the couch, her chest heaving. The fabric scratched at her skin, a reminder of the chasm that now lay between them. In the stillness of the living room, the tension hung heavy, a tangible thing that wrapped around her like a shroud. She had many questions and a lot of insecurities, but one thing was for certain.

She was no fool.

Chapter 21

I swung open the heavy wooden door of The Coffee House, the tinkling chime announcing my arrival. The warm, inviting lights illuminated the cozy place, and the aroma of freshly brewed coffee enveloped me like a warm hug. Diane was already seated in a booth, her beauty radiating like a beacon, even in the dim lighting.

"Hello," I said with a smile as I slid into the seat across from her.

"Hi, Eva Rae," she replied, her sharp eyes taking in every detail of my appearance. We quickly placed our orders—blueberry muffins and two cups of steaming black coffee for me and a creamy concoction with sugar for Diane.

"Spill it," Diane prompted before our order even hit the table. "There's no hiding that something is going on. You look distressed."

The waitress brought over our coffee. Steam curled from the cups like ghosts of my thoughts. I took a gulp, scalding my tongue but barely noticing. I needed more. I poured in sugar. My fingers fumbled with a spoon, twirling it aimlessly.

"Everything okay?" Her voice cut through the hum of low conversations and the occasional hiss from the espresso machine. Concern lined her face, softening the edges of her usually composed features.

"Uh, yeah," I lied. With another swig of coffee, the mug emptied too soon. "Can I get a refill?" I called to the waitress, my voice sharper than intended.

Diane reached across the table, her hand hovering as if to steady mine. "Eva Rae, talk to me."

Her words were a tether, and for a moment, I clung to them, trying to ground myself in the familiarity of our friendship. But the storm inside wouldn't let up, and I knew it was only a matter of time before it broke loose.

The refill arrived, a steaming torrent splashing into my mug. I clasped it for energy, the ceramic radiating against my clammy palms. I leaned in, the words tumbling from me in a hushed avalanche.

"I've been up all night, Diane. Carol Rudolph—Will and Angela's neighbor—was found dead. In her house. Actually, I was the one who found her."

My eyes met hers, pleading for understanding.

"Dead? How so?"

"She was bludgeoned. It was ugly. Blood everywhere… And the cops… they grilled me for hours."

Her face drained of color, her poised demeanor crumbling like a cliffside in slow motion.

"Me, Diane. They think I might be involved because I was there. For all I know, they might think I murdered her."

Diane's fingers twitched around her cup, the polished surface now a lifeline as she absorbed the gravity of my confession. Her blue eyes, always so steady, flickered with a storm of emotions.

"Murder?" The word was barely audible over the clatter of cups and chatter. "Eva Rae, this is… you can't be serious."

I nodded, each movement heavy with fatigue and an acute awareness of the stakes. The silverware on our table seemed to rattle with the intensity of my heartbeat.

"Dead serious," I said, my voice laced with concern and urgency. My gaze locked onto hers, willing her to grasp the full weight of the situation.

Diane's hands trembled, just perceptibly, betraying the shock that had seized her composure. She looked at me, not as the confident Diane I knew, but as someone confronted with a reality too stark to fully comprehend.

"Carol…," she whispered, her voice trailing off into the ambient noise of the coffee house, her thoughts lost amid the scent of roasted beans and the soft jazz playing in the background. "I remember her well. Angela thought for a long time that Will had an affair with her. She never liked her."

I reached for the muffin, breaking off a piece more out of habit than hunger. Diane was still gripping her coffee cup like a lifeline.

"Did Angela ever mention anything about prescription drugs?" I kept my voice low and gentle despite the urgency scratching at my insides. "Her husband… was he addicted?"

For a moment, Diane's composure wavered. Her eyes slid away from mine, seeking refuge in the abstract patterns of the coffee house floor. Then, with an effort that seemed to pull her back into the present, her gaze lifted, locking with mine, a silent admission before words even formed.

"Yes," she said, her voice a mere whisper. "Angela told me… about the drugs."

The air between us thickened, laden with unsaid implications and secrets that now began to seep through the cracks of a carefully constructed facade.

I leaned forward, the booth's vinyl squeaking beneath me. A strand of red hair escaped my ponytail, brushing against my cheek as I spoke in a conspiratorial whisper.

"Diane, in Angela's notebook, there were notes. About Will. She was describing erratic behavior. I spoke to my medical expert back in Cocoa Beach, and he confirmed that this type of drug can change a man's behavior and make him aggressive. I need to know if this was the case. Did Will show signs of erratic behavior?"

My words hung in the air, mingling with the scent of espresso and cinnamon from someone's latte at the next table.

"Erratic?" Diane's voice was barely audible above the hiss of the steamer. Her face, moments ago flushed with the warmth of our booth, now drained to an ashen hue. Her hands, resting on the table, trembled ever so slightly.

"Yes. It raises questions." My eyes stayed locked on hers, searching, probing for any flicker of acknowledgment or any sign she recognized the man described on those pages.

Diane inhaled sharply. Her blue eyes swelled with something akin to fear, or maybe it was disbelief. Disbelief tinged with the faintest trace of betrayal.

"Diane, Angela wrote in her notebook that she was scared of him. Of him either hurting himself or someone else."

"He didn't kill her," she said, the words tumbling out like a plea. "Especially not over some… silly drug addiction."

The conviction in her tone clashed with the uncertainty in her gaze. She wanted to believe it, needed to believe it. Her son-in-law, the father of her grandchildren—surely he couldn't be capable of murder.

"Of course," I replied, my response measured, but my mind racing. The pieces weren't fitting together, and every new revelation seemed only to deepen the mystery surrounding Carol's death.

The server approached, refilling our coffees with a clink of porcelain on porcelain, oblivious to the tension. I thanked him with a nod, watching Diane compose herself once more, the mask of certainty sliding back into place.

I tapped the table, my fingers drumming a staccato rhythm that mirrored the beat of my racing heart.

"Did Angela ever share worries about Will's behavior with you?" The question hung in the air, a thread waiting to be pulled.

Diane's posture wilted slightly, the corners of her eyes crinkling with the weight of a mother's sorrow.

"No," she sighed, her voice carrying the burden of remembrance. "Angela fretted over him cheating, not… violence."

"I heard this about her before; can you elaborate?"

"She became obsessed over it." Diane's fingers traced the rim of her coffee cup, tracing invisible patterns. "She saw hints, signs of infidelity everywhere."

"Everywhere?" I leaned in closer, my curiosity piqued by the fervor in Diane's description.

"Even when there were none," Diane confirmed, a droplet of sadness falling from her words. Her blue eyes seemed to look past me, focusing on a painful point in time only she could see.

I leaned back, the worn leather of the booth creaking under my shifting weight. My mind was a cyclone of doubt and suspicion, each thought colliding with another, leaving me questioning everything I thought I knew. There had to be more hidden layers yet to be uncovered.

"Will loved her," Diane murmured, breaking into my whirling thoughts. She stretched across the table, her hand warm against the chill of my arm. "He wouldn't… he couldn't have done this. I knew my daughter. She could be a lot from time to time. Her obsession with him cheating… it drove her nuts."

"Love can be complex," I said, not quite ready to dispel the fog of theories shrouding my brain.

"Complex, yes, but not deadly. At least not in this case." Her eyes held mine, pleading for understanding. "His addiction, it's true—it took him to dark places. But not to murder. And not to betrayal."

"Accidents happen," I conceded, the words tasting bitter as they left my mouth.

"Angela's death was tragic, but an accident," Diane insisted, her grip tightening. "Stairs can be… they're treacherous."

"Treacherous," I echoed, the term snagging on something within me, a detail, perhaps, or an intuition I could not yet articulate.

"Please," she continued, her voice a soft lilt of hope amidst the cacophony of my skepticism, "you have to see that Will isn't capable of such horror."

Her conviction was a beacon in the fog, but did it illuminate the truth or cast shadows where clarity needed to reign?

"Thank you, Diane," I said, my words measured against the torrent of thoughts inside my head. "I appreciate you being here."

The coffee house was a blur of motion and chatter around me, but it all seemed distant, secondary to the

DARK LITTLE SERETCS

puzzle pieces floating in my mind. Her support was a lifeline, yet doubt gnawed at me, a relentless itch.

"Anytime, Eva Rae." Her voice held the warmth of a summer's embrace, but I was out in the cold, sorting through the frost of facts and speculation.

"Truth has a way of surfacing," I murmured more to myself than to her, standing up from the booth with an abruptness that mirrored my urgency.

"Find it then," she said, her eyes following me as I slid out of the booth. "But find the real truth. We don't have much time. Will's trial starts tomorrow."

"I know," I said, feeling defeated. The little I had wasn't exactly enough. "I will get to the bottom of this."

I rose to my feet, the promise lingering behind me. I felt like I was lying to her. I didn't see how I would be able to find anything before tomorrow that would help Will. I wanted to help Diane; I truly did. And I wanted to find out what really happened to Angela and, of course, Carol. Why did she have to die? Was it the same killer?

The bell above the coffee shop door jingled sharply as I pushed through, stepping into the daylight. The sun was too bright, too cheery for the grim task ahead. My pace quickened, every step a beat in the symphony of my racing heart.

Will's addiction, Angela's fears, Carol's death—all whispered secrets carried on the breeze that brushed past me.

With each block passed while driving, my resolve hardened. Carol's lifeless eyes haunted me, a silent plea. I needed answers. I needed to peel back the layers of deception until nothing remained but the stark, unyielding reality.

I took a deep breath, the weight of unsolved mysteries heavy on my shoulders. It was up to me to uncover the truth. Was it murder? An accident? Or an affair gone wrong? The words swirled in my mind like menacing vultures.

But I couldn't stop now. Carol deserved more, and I would stop at nothing to bring it to her, even if it meant delving deeper into the dark secrets of this sweltering Florida town.

Who could I trust? I wasn't sure anymore.

Chapter 22

I stopped my car in front of Carol's house, its windows dark and unwelcoming. The hum of the engine died as I turned the key, leaving nothing but silence—very different to the chaos I had stumbled upon there the night before. The forensic team was gone; their vanishing act as meticulous as the evidence markers they left behind.

Slipping under the yellow tape felt like stepping over a threshold into another world—a crime scene frozen in time. My footsteps on the wooden floorboards echoed up the stairwell, a haunting reminder that I was walking back into a nightmare.

The upstairs hall was a gallery of numbered tags and stickers. Every inch had been documented, cataloged, and now abandoned by the forensics team. But the bedroom—the epicenter of violence—was where the story screamed loudest.

As I stepped through the doorway, the disarray hit me. Drawers yanked from dressers, clothes strewn like casualties of some domestic war. A lamp lay shattered, its light extinguished forever, just like Carol's. The bed was unmade, pillows tossed aside with reckless abandon. And there, amidst it all, was the dark stain on the carpet. The spot where Carol had breathed her last, where I found her lying still and silent.

My heart sank at the sight, a leaden weight in my chest. The room was a chaotic canvas; each overturned chair and each scattered paper was a brushstroke in a macabre masterpiece or a bizarre horror show. It was as though the killer had choreographed a dance of destruction, leaving behind a maelstrom of clues—or perhaps a deliberate lack thereof. It was obvious Carol had fought for her life until the end.

I moved carefully around the space, respectful of the invisible fingerprints the forensics team had sought to capture. Yellow tape crisscrossed the room, segmenting it into a grid of tragedy. Evidence markers stood sentinel, guarding the silent testimony of the deceased.

The gravity of the situation bore down on me, the tension in the air almost palpable. Carol's life had ended here, violently, senselessly. And somewhere out there, someone carried the weight of her death on their conscience—if they had one at all.

I took pictures of it all, planning on studying them later, hoping to find some answer or even just a clue. I took a deep breath, willing my racing thoughts to slow. Justice was a puzzle, and this was another piece. Now it was time to see where it fit, to draw connections in a web of lies and secrets. Carol's killer was still out there, but I was closer now, the trail fresh and beckoning.

With one last look at the room that held too many answers and yet not enough, I backed away. I left the ruins of Carol's last moments behind, carrying the weight of what happened here and what was yet to be uncovered.

There was work to be done, and I would not rest until the truth was dragged into the light.

My pulse hammered in my ears as I paced down the corridor, each footstep echoing against the sterile quiet like a drumbeat of impending revelation. The stillness of the house felt unnatural… as if the very walls were holding their breath.

I halted at Carol's office door, framed by flapping crime scene tape that felt like accusatory fingers pointing right at my chest. There was a magnetic pull to this space, an unspoken promise that within these four walls lay fragments of truth waiting to be unearthed.

"Just a quick look, Eva Rae," I whispered to myself, steeling my nerves. My hand hovered briefly before pushing the door open with a soft creak that seemed too loud and intrusive in the silent house.

The air inside Carol's office hung thick. Every surface appeared untouched, even though the forensics team had swept through, leaving behind only the scent of antiseptic sprays and latent despair.

My eyes darted across the room, instinctively cataloging potential clues.

"Keep looking," I chided myself, directing my attention to the chaos atop the mahogany desk. Papers littered the surface, some face-up, displaying half-finished sentences and numbers that could have meant anything—or nothing at all. Carol was an accountant. Her entire life was numbers. Her computer was gone and would be scrutinized by the forensics IT team. But it would take time. I was looking for something fast to help me right here and now.

My fingers trembled slightly as they sifted through the documents, seeking the jagged edge of an anomaly among the mundane.

Photographs in the drawers, invoices, letters… each snippet felt like a piece of a puzzle that refused to fit together.

"Come on, there's got to be something here."

The words tumbled out softly, a mantra to keep the creeping frustration at bay. Scan, sort, analyze—my mind shifted into the methodical rhythm of the hunt, allowing intuition to guide the dance of logic and gut feeling.

"Where are you?" I murmured, almost pleading with the inanimate objects to reveal their secrets. Time was slipping away, but the puzzle beckoned, promising revelation just beyond the reach of my fingertips.

"Patience," I reminded myself. "Determination." These were the tools of my trade, honed through years of chasing shadows and wrestling with enigmas. This room, Carol's last stronghold of privacy, would not defy me for long. I would find the thread that unraveled the mystery, even if it meant sifting through a thousand innocuous scraps to grasp it.

My fingers paused mid-riffle, the tips brushing over a corner of paper that didn't belong. It was wedged between legal pads and expense reports from three years ago, incongruent in its texture. I pulled it out, heart thumping against my ribs.

"Hello, what's this?" The whisper felt loud in the silence,

My eyes narrowed as I scanned the documents, stopping on one that sent a chill down my spine. I could barely believe it.

"Gotcha," I breathed. The room seemed to close in, walls inching nearer with the gravity of my find. "This changes everything."

I clutched the paper like a lifeline, suddenly aware of my isolated presence in the dead woman's office. This wasn't just another breadcrumb; it was the loaf, the bakery, the whole damn baking industry.

I slid the document into my pocket, feeling its weight like a stone. The implications were massive, tendrils of consequence reaching into dark corners I hadn't even considered. If I was right about this—and my gut screamed that I was—things had changed massively.

"Careful, Eva Rae," I cautioned myself, voice barely above a hum. "This is bigger than you anticipated."

With the document secured, I took one last scan of the room, ensuring nothing else was amiss. The air seemed to pulse with my accelerated heartbeat, each throb a stark reminder of what lay ahead.

The room fell silent again as I stepped out, leaving behind the chaos of papers, the echo of my discovery hanging in the stillness.

Shadows clung to the walls like specters of doubt, but they couldn't touch the clarity taking shape within me. This was bigger than I'd imagined, a web with strands crossing into uncharted territories of power and malice.

I slipped under the crime scene tape, a barrier that felt more symbolic now than practical. Outside, the evening air brushed against my skin, a contrast to the stifling tension left behind within those walls.

"Who would have thought?" I caught myself speaking to the wind, a half-hearted chuckle escaping despite the gravity nipping at my heels. "Pandora's box, sitting in a drawer."

The last look I took imprinted the scene in my memory—a photograph of potential leads, unanswered questions, and a trail of deceit I was hell-bent on unraveling. The pool of blood, now a fading stain beneath the moon's watchful eye, whispered of secrets spilled and lives shattered.

I walked back to my car, the engine's hum a companion to the cacophony of thoughts racing for attention. As I drove off, the rearview mirror captured the retreating silhouette of Carol's house, a chapter closing only to crack open the next—where the true work began.

SCATTERED notes and photos sprawled across the Airbnb's dining table, each piece a fragment of a larger, darker puzzle. I leaned over them, my brain churning as I drew lines from one suspect to another, dates to events, whispers to shouts. Truth was there... lurking in the shadows cast by the lamplight, waiting for me to snatch it from obscurity.

I shuffled through the papers, my fingertips brushing over the surface of Carol's life and death. The players involved, their motives interwoven in a tapestry so complex it almost seemed impossible. A timeline took shape before me, a sinuous path that promised to help me get to the truth.

The timeline was the key.

Hours ticked away, blurring into a haze of determination and caffeine. My eyes grew heavy, but surrender wasn't an option.

"Enough," I finally conceded, muscles protesting as I stood. Tomorrow would bring new resolve. I shuffled the evidence into neat stacks and closed my computer, where a bunch of emails from Matt were the last things I had opened. I was proud of us working as a team again. He had helped me get clarity about some things that would be brought into daylight in the morning.

In the bathroom, the mirror held a reflection tinged with fatigue. Green eyes met mine, more resolute than ever.

"You've got this," I told the woman staring back at me. "Face down the darkness."

A splash of cold water, and the face looking back seemed less weary, more fierce. My red hair lay damp against my forehead. I turned away, leaving my reflection to its silent vigil.

The bedroom was a haven of soft sheets and promises of sleep. I slipped under the covers, the fabric cool against skin that still remembered the heat of Florida's sun. My mind raced, weaving through the labyrinth of deceit and danger, but my heart… my heart was steady.

Sleep reached for me, a gentle tide pulling at the edges of consciousness. And as I drifted off, I clung to the lifeline of that purpose, the certainty that I was the key to unlocking the truth.

Chapter 23

THEN:

Angela's gaze clung to the scene unfolding beyond the sheer curtains of the living room window. Will, her husband, stood just outside, his silhouette casting a long shadow across the freshly cut grass. They had made up from their last fight. It had been good for a while, but Angela kept her eyes open. Her friend Sam told her to look for someone closer to home instead of dating apps and social media. Now, she was staring at precisely that— someone very close to her home… too close. Carol, their neighbor, approached Will with a stride that suggested a casual encounter, but Angela's intuition prickled with unease.

"Hey, Will!" Carol's voice was light and airy.

"Carol, nice to see you," Will replied, his tone friendly yet reserved.

Angela watched, her heart drumming as Carol tilted her head back, laughter spilling from her lips at something

Will had said. She stepped closer to him, her body language open and inviting.

Too darn inviting.

The sun glinted off Carol's auburn hair, igniting it like autumn leaves in an October sun. She reached out, her fingers brushing against Will's arm in a touch that lingered. It was subtle, perhaps meaningless to an unobservant eye. But Angela saw. She felt each feather-light contact like a weight dropping into her stomach.

"Really?" Carol said, her hand resting a beat too long on his bicep. "That's hilarious."

Angela's breath caught. The air in the room seemed too thin, her fingers tightening on the windowsill's edge. Will chuckled, shifting his weight, but he did not step back. Not immediately.

Carol leaned in, her shoulder nearly brushing against Will's. Her smile was wide, teeth gleaming white against her red lipstick. Her voice dipped lower, words lost to Angela, but the message was clear.

Intimate. Private.

What the heck? Right in front of me?

Angela's pulse pounded in her ears, every flirtatious gesture by Carol amplifying the cacophony of suspicion in her mind. The touching. The leaning. The proximity that screamed more than neighborly friendliness.

Will finally put a subtle space between them, a gentle barrier. Yet Carol's eyes locked onto his, unyielding, conveying a silent challenge that tore through Angela's composure. Angela's throat tightened, each breath a battle as she fought the urge to shatter the glassy barrier that kept her a silent spectator to this unfolding play of potential betrayal.

The door slammed behind her, and the sound was a sharp crack that split the air. Angela's heart thundered against her ribs as she stalked across the lawn, eyes locked on the two figures entwined in conversation. Her shadow stretched long and angry over the manicured grass.

"Carol!" The name erupted from her lips, a bullet shot from a gun.

Carol turned, surprise etching her features for a fleeting second before she schooled her face into a mask of innocence. Will swiveled, his expression one of confusion that shifted quickly to concern.

"Angela, what—?"

"Stay away from him," Angela spat, cutting through Will's words like a knife slicing silk. She was close now—too close, her finger jabbing toward Carol's chest with an accusing zeal.

"Trying to steal my husband?" Her voice climbed, a crescendo of fury. "Right in front of me?"

"Angela, please—" Will reached out, but she pulled away.

"Will, talk some sense into her; she's out of control," Carol said, but Angela barely registered the plea. Her focus narrowed to the woman before her, the perceived threat that sent adrenaline coursing through her veins.

"Stay away from Will," Angela repeated, each word a hammer pounding the finality of her command. Her breaths came fast and shallow, painting the autumn chill with the heat of her rage.

"Or you'll regret it."

Carol's hands lifted, a barrier to the onslaught. "Angela, this isn't what it looks like. We were just—"

"Chatting?" Angela's laugh was brittle, jagged. "I'm not blind, Carol."

"Really, it's not—" Carol's protest withered under Angela's glare.

"Save it." Angela stepped closer, voice low and menacing. "I see how you look at him."

"Angela…."

"Shut up!" The command sliced through Carol's feeble defense and severed it clean. Her voice boomed now, unrecognizable even to her own ears—a tempest unleashed. "You think I don't notice? The 'casual' touches, the sly glances?"

"Angela, please—" Carol's eyes darted, seeking an escape that wasn't there.

"Stay away from my family." Each word was a bullet, precise and lethal. "Stay away from my life."

"Angela, listen to me," Carol implored, but her words evaporated in the raw heat of Angela's fury.

"Or what?" Angela's voice crescendoed, a violent wave crashing against the shore. "You'll what, Carol?"

"Nothing! I swear, Angela—"

"Swear on what? Your deceit?" Angela's scorn was palpable, thick in the air between them. "I don't want your empty promises."

"Angela, no threats are necessary," Carol tried, a tremor in her voice betraying her composure.

"Threats?" Angela's laugh was dark, humorless. "No, these are promises, Carol. Promises."

"Angela…." Carol backtracked a step, a silent plea for reprieve.

"Stay. Away." The finality in Angela's tone left no room for argument, an iron-clad decree as she towered over Carol, an avenging fury in human form.

"Enough." Will's hand was on Angela's shoulder, a firm yet gentle weight. "Angela, come back inside."

She spun, her blue eyes alight with the fire of betrayal. "You're defending her?" Her voice was a whip, each word stinging.

"Defending? No, I'm—" Will's gaze flickered between the two women, seeking a foothold in the maelstrom.

"Allowing," she spat the word as if it were venom. "Allowing her to worm her way into our lives."

"Angela, you're seeing things that aren't there." His words, meant to be soothing, only fueled the flames.

"Seeing? Or do you just wish I was blind to it?" Her chest heaved with the force of her breaths, an accusing finger pointed squarely at him now.

"Please, let's go inside and talk about this," Will pleaded, his voice tight, laced with urgency.

"Talk?" She laughed, cold and bitter. "Like you 'talk' with Carol?"

"Angela, stop this!" Will's hands held her arms, but his grip faltered under the sheer heat of her anger.

"Stop protecting her!" She shook free, eyes never leaving his, a silent demand for truth.

"Protecting? I am not—" He struggled for composure, his plea dissolving into the chill of the coming night.

"Angela, you know I would never do anything to hurt you," Will's voice cracked like thin ice beneath heavy steps, his eyes searching hers for some sign of the trust they once shared.

"Wouldn't you?" Angela's retort cut through the thick air, each word a shard of glass. "Then why is it always her?"

"Always her? You're not being fair." He shook his head, the lines of stress etched across his brow deepening.

"Fair?" She scoffed, her laugh sharp and hollow. "And what about me, Will? What is fair about this, about feeling second in my own home?"

"Second? That's not how it is." His defense was swift, but his voice wavered, betraying him. "We barely ever talk."

"Isn't it?" Her voice rose, a crescendo of pain and betrayal. "Isn't it, Will?"

"Listen to yourself, Angela! This is madness!" Will's hands flailed, grasping at the remnants of their normalcy.

"Madness?" She echoed, her face contorted with anguish. "No, this is clarity! It's seeing things exactly as they are. I've been blind for so long. God, have I been blind."

"Please, Ange—" he reached out, but she recoiled as if from a flame.

"Don't!" She stepped back, arms wrapped around herself as though holding the pieces of her heart together. "Just don't."

"Angela, this isn't you," Will implored, his voice edged with desperation now.

"Isn't me?" Tears glistened in Angela's eyes, her breath coming in ragged gasps. "Or is it just not the me you want to see?"

"Angela…." The word was a plea, a lifeline thrown into churning waters.

"Enough," she breathed, a whisper that held the weight of finality. "Just enough."

Will watched, helpless, as she turned away, leaving behind a silence that spoke volumes.

Back inside, Angela's fists clenched, nails digging crescents into her palms. Her breath became erratic. The house loomed around her, walls whispering secrets, each family portrait a mocking jeer. She was pacing back and forth on the Persian rug that had witnessed better days. Her heart thrummed a chaotic rhythm, every beat screaming betrayal.

No wonder Will wouldn't sleep with her. He slept with Carol, didn't he? That's why. That was why he refused her all the time. How long had this been going on? Years?

"Angela," Will's voice cut through the fog of her thoughts as he closed the door with a soft click. He approached her, his footsteps hesitant.

"Stay back," she spat without turning, her voice a serrated blade.

"Please, let me explain," he implored, reaching for her shoulder.

She whirled around, shrugging off his touch like a shroud of flames. "Explain? Your lies are clear enough!"

"Angie, it's not what you think," Will's words tumbled out, desperate to bridge the chasm between them. "She's our neighbor. I was just being friendly."

"Isn't it what I think?" Angela countered, eyes ablaze, searching his face for a sliver of truth in an ocean of deceit. "You must take me for a fool."

"Believe me." His hands were up now, pleading. "I love you."

"Love?" A hollow laugh escaped her. "Your 'love' is a poison."

"Angela, stop this," he tried to steady her with a touch, but she recoiled, feeling like a wounded animal cornered by its predator.

"Stop? You've torn us apart!" Her voice surged, each word punctuated by the hammering of her pulse.

"Let me help—" Will's plea strangled as he reached for her again.

"Help?" Angela jerked away, tears welling, threatening to spill. "You've done enough."

"Angie, I'm here for you, for us," he persisted, voice quivering on the edge of despair.

"Us?" she echoed, the word foreign, tainted. "There is no 'us' in betrayal."

"Listen to me!" Will's command was more a broken

whisper than an authoritative directive. "What do you want me to do? I am being totally honest about my addiction with you. Yet you seem to think I'm always hiding something. You're constantly asking me about receipts for restaurants I barely remember going to or why I changed my passwords somewhere when it was because I was asked to or because I had forgotten them. You call me at work constantly, and if I don't answer, you immediately spin some crazy story about me doing God only knows what when I'm actually attending to patients, which is my job. You gotta stop this insane behavior, Angela. You have to listen to me."

"Listening's overrated," she hissed, turning away from him, from their life splintering at the seams.

"Angela, please," he begged, one last attempt to salvage the wreckage.

"Save your breath, Will." Her shoulders stiffened, a fortress wall against his entreaties. "Just save it."

Her stride carried her through the tempest of emotion, each step a declaration, leaving Will to grapple with the silence that swallowed his pleas whole.

Angela's back slammed against the hallway wall, her breaths shallow and rapid. She slid down, knees buckling, hands trembling as they sought the cool solidity of the floorboards. The house echoed with the residue of their argument, each thud of her heartbeat a reminder of the discord.

"Angie." Will's voice scratched the charged air, barely louder than a whisper.

"Leave me be," she managed through gritted teeth.

He hovered, a specter of concern, his shadow merging with the fading light. "This isn't us."

"Isn't it?" Her voice was venom, laced with disbelief. The notion of "us" had become a cruel joke.

"Please," he implored, kneeling at arm's length, reaching out only with his gaze.

"Enough," Angela spat, the word sharp, a shard of glass. She pushed to her feet, ignoring the dizziness that swam around her.

"Angela—" His plea cut short as she held up a hand, silencing him.

"Silent house, silent vows," she muttered, a mantra to keep the fury at bay. Her eyes swept the room, once a sanctuary, now tainted—memories distorted by suspicion's ugly hue. The kids were in their rooms. She didn't want them to see her like this.

"Talk to me." Will's voice cracked, his form blurred by the tears she refused to shed.

"Angela, we can—"

"Can we?" Skepticism dripped from her lips, her glance slicing through his unfinished sentence.

"Damn it, listen!" He rose, frustration etching lines into his once-familiar face.

"Listening's done." She turned away, her movement deliberate, a slow burn in a sea of chaos. She ran away from him.

"Where are you going?" Desperation tinged his voice, but she was already past hearing.

"Somewhere quiet," she said, half to herself, craving the silence that promised no lies, no whispers of betrayal.

"Angela!" His call was a tether she severed with the closing of the door behind her.

The bedroom welcomed her with open arms, a false comfort in its unchanged appearance. Clothes lay folded, and pictures smiled from their frames, but the air was different—thick with words unsaid, feelings unmet.

The mirror caught her reflection, a stranger with eyes like storm clouds, charged with electricity yet to strike.

She breathed in and out, a rhythm seeking calm amidst the turmoil. The anger hummed beneath her skin, a live wire without an outlet.

"Steady now," she whispered, fists clenching and unclenching, willing the anger to subside, to give way to clarity.

"Angela?" Will's voice seeped through the wood, cautious, a knock softer than a heartbeat.

"Go away," she called back, her tone a barrier he couldn't breach.

"Angie, I'm sorry," his words muffled, an offering laid at the altar of their love.

"Sorry doesn't patch holes," she replied, cold, resolute.

"Let me in," he persisted, the doorknob jiggling gently.

"I locked it," she stated, flat. Not just the door, but her heart too, encased in ice.

"Please," he tried again, his presence a weight against the other side.

"Goodnight, Will," she said, finality lacing the farewell, the evening sun casting long shadows across the bed.

"Angela…."

"Goodnight," she repeated, stronger, a full stop to their day's tumultuous sentence.

The house settled around her, creaks and groans of a structure strained, mirroring the tension that clung to her like a second skin. Silence enveloped her, a temporary reprieve, but under the calm surface, her anger simmered, unresolved, threatening to boil over once more.

Chapter 24

The heavy doors swung open, a silent herald to my purposeful strides. The courtroom's solemn air wrapped around me, the weight of expectation pressing against my chest. I scanned the room—a sea of stern faces, a judge perched like an omniscient observer, and a jury cloaked in civic duty.

Will Jennings sat at the defense table, his polished exterior a stark contrast to the tension that rippled through his frame. Our eyes met. I approached, heels clicking on the courtroom floor, each step measured, resounding through the silence. As I drew nearer, a brief nod passed between us—a silent exchange of solidarity. He exhaled softly, a ghost of a smile tugging at his lips, acknowledging the unspoken vow hanging in the air.

"Let's get this over with," I whispered, more to myself than to him.

His gaze held mine for a moment longer. "Thank you, Eva Rae," he murmured almost imperceptibly.

I turned away from him, facing forward, ready for battle.

The prosecutor's voice sliced through the courtroom, clinical and detached. "Ladies and gentlemen of the jury, Carol Rudolph saw it all. She witnessed Will Jennings, in a fit of rage, push his wife Angela down the stairs—a fatal act."

A collective breath seemed to be held, the jury leaning in as if on cue, hanging onto every word that painted Will as a cold-blooded spouse slayer.

"Murder," the prosecutor pronounced with finality, "plain and simple."

I felt my pulse quicken, adrenaline surging as I prepared to dismantle their case brick by brick. My fingers brushed over the neatly stacked evidence at my side. The moment had come, and it was mine to seize.

"Your Honor," I said, standing. My voice didn't waver; it rang out, commanding the room. "I have compelling evidence that calls for immediate dismissal of this case."

The courtroom hushed. Even the air seemed to pause, waiting.

"Objection," sounded from the prosecutor. "She's not his lawyer."

"Who are you?" the judge asked.

I held up my badge. "FBI Agent Eva Rae Thomas. I've been looking into this case for some time now."

"Your honor, she can't just"

The judge held up a hand to stop him, and he sat back down.

"I'll allow it," the judge said. "But it better be good."

"It is, Your Honor," I said.

I held up the plane tickets first—crisp, undeniable proof. "These are plane tickets for Carol Rudolph for a flight to New York City, dated May 14th, three years ago." I let that sink in, then placed them decisively on the bench in front of me.

"Furthermore," I continued, confidence peaking as I switched on my laptop and turned it so they could see, "this is video surveillance from JFK Airport showing Ms. Rudolph on the day before Angela Jennings' supposed murder."

The footage, unyielding in its truth, flickered to life on the wall behind me, Carol Rudolph unmistakable among throngs of travelers.

"Why is this important?" I pivoted to face the jury, their eyes wide, fixated. "Because the entire case hinges on her testimony that she saw Will push his wife on the morning of May 15, three years ago."

I paused, letting the gravity of my words permeate the space.

"Carol Rudolph claimed she kept silent out of love for Will, only coming forward recently, leading to his arrest." Now, it was time for the knockout blow. "But she couldn't have seen anything. She wasn't even in the state, let alone outside the house."

I could feel the shift in the room, the scales of justice quivering under the weight of truth.

"Her social media pages? Scrubbed clean of any evidence of her trip. But thanks to Detective Matt Miller's cyber expertise, we retrieved the deleted content." I gestured toward the screen where photos of Carol in New York popped up, timestamped and undeniable. One of them was taken on the evening of May 15 at a rooftop bar.

"Here they are," I declared, letting the evidence speak for itself, my voice the vessel of vindication as the courtroom erupted into a cacophony of whispers and shuffling papers.

"Miss Thomas, while your digital exhibition is compelling," the prosecutor began, his voice laced with skepticism, "it's hardly conclusive. Deleted social media photos do not a solid alibi make."

"Your Honor," I countered without missing a beat, "the time-stamped evidence directly contradicts the prosecution's key witness testimony. It's not just about pictures—it's about where Miss Rudolph was—and wasn't. There is evidence of her being in New York City on May 15th and 16th. There is no way she could have been in St. Augustine on the night of the 15th. The surveillance cameras at JFK show her returning on the 20th."

The defense attorney stood, seizing the moment. "If I may, Your Honor, the integrity of the prosecution's case is compromised. We have incontrovertible proof that their witness was almost a thousand miles away when she claimed to be an eyewitness to murder."

"Objection, Your Honor!" the prosecutor shot back. "This so-called proof is nothing but a digital smokescreen. There's no telling what trickery could've been used to manipulate this information."

"As I said, I have the tickets here," I said and held them up. "Carol Rudolph was an accountant and kept all kinds of proof of her whereabouts so she could deduct trips and visits to restaurants. She would keep them for five years as the IRS requires."

"Objection overruled," the judge stated firmly, focusing on the printouts and screen still displaying Carol's images against the backdrop of New York City landmarks: the Empire State Building, Central Park, and the Statue of Liberty. It was all there, thanks to Matt.

I watched as he scrutinized each piece, his brow furrowed in concentration. He picked up the plane tickets, his fingers tracing the flight details before moving on to the video surveillance playback, his eyes narrowing at the sequence of events unfolding before him.

Silence clung to the courtroom like a second skin as the judge leaned back in his chair, eyes hooded beneath heavy brows. His gaze shifted methodically—first to me, Eva Rae, my heart thrumming against my ribcage, then to the evidence displayed on screens and strewn in front of him. It lingered there on the timestamps and images that challenged the prosecution's narrative.

From the corner of my eye, I saw Diane Matthews, her hands clenched in her lap, lips pressed into a thin line. Will Jennings sat rigid, the muscles in his jaw twitching with barely concealed anxiety. The air was thick with expectation; every spectator seemed to hold their breath, waiting for the verdict that would change lives.

The judge's fingers tapped a silent rhythm on the wooden gavel, a beat that seemed to echo the pounding of my own pulse. He glanced at the jury, their faces a mosaic of doubt and contemplation before his eyes fixed once more on the evidence that held the power to shatter the prosecution's case.

"Your Honor," the prosecutor began, but the judge raised a hand, silencing him mid-plea.

"Enough," he stated, his voice resonating through the stillness. "This court has heard and seen sufficient argument and evidence."

The room contracted as if in anticipation, the walls themselves leaning in closer. His hand gripped the gavel, knuckles whitening, and with one swift, deliberate motion, it came crashing down.

"Dr. Will Jennings," the judge announced, his tone devoid of emotion yet carrying an undercurrent of finality, "this court finds you not guilty of the murder of Angela Jennings."

A collective gasp rippled through the courtroom; it was the sound of a storm breaking. Shock etched itself onto the faces of the prosecution while a surge of relief washed over Diane, her blue eyes brimming with tears that reflected light like shards of glass. Will's expression morphed from tension to disbelief, as if the words he had just heard were in a foreign language.

"Order!" the judge commanded as murmurs swelled into a cacophony. But inside that chaos was a clear note of victory, a melody that sang of justice served.

I stood there, my own relief a quiet shadow amidst the uproar, already feeling the pull of unanswered questions tugging at the edge of my mind. The chapter had closed, but the story, my story, was far from over.

A scuffle at the back of the courtroom snagged my attention. Detective Larson, a shadow since the trial began, now moved with haste, his form slinking between the bodies standing to applaud or gape. His eyes, quicksilver and shifty, met mine for a heartbeat before skittering away.

"Excuse me," he muttered, shoulders hunched as if to ward off the weight of countless stares that didn't come. The door closed behind him with a click too soft for such an abrupt exit.

You can run, but you cannot hide.

"Diane!" Will's voice broke through my focus on the retreating detective.

I swung around just in time to see Diane fling herself into her son-in-law's arms. They held each other with a fierceness born from years of shared pain, their relief tangible, a living thing that pulsed through the room. People, family, and friends shuffled around them, their own dramas forgotten momentarily in the face of such raw emotion.

"Thank you, Eva Rae," Diane whispered, her voice a thread of silk in a field of thorns. She pulled back just enough to allow her gratitude to spill over into her embrace. "You brought him back to us. To his children."

"Couldn't have done it without you," I said, meaning every word.

Will's gaze found mine over Diane's shoulder, a silent thank you shared in that look.

I leaned against the cool marble wall, a silent sentinel to the jubilation that unfolded before me. Diane and Will's embrace was a freeze-frame of victory and vindication, their smiles beacons in the dimly lit courtroom. Yet my heart harbored a thrum of unease, the detective's furtive escape etching shadows across my mind.

"Remarkable work, Eva Rae," a colleague murmured, clapping me on the shoulder, but I barely registered the praise. My gaze lingered on the space the detective had vacated, the ghost of his nervous energy still palpable in the air. What was he hiding? Why did he run?

I had a feeling I knew.

"Thanks," I replied, my voice distant, eyes not leaving the corner where the detective had disappeared.

Diane caught my eye, her smile faltering as she read the concern etched in my expression.

"Eva Rae?" she questioned, the joy in her voice ebbing into worry.

"Nothing's over yet," I said, more to myself than to her. The words left a bitter taste; there was more to unearth, rot running deeper than this courtroom drama.

"Will's free because of you," Diane pressed, willing me to share in the moment.

"Free, yes. But the truth—is still shackled," I countered, my thoughts racing faster than my ability to articulate them. Angela's death might have been an accident, but Carol's definitely wasn't."

"Where are you going?" Will called out as I started for the exit, every step brimming with purpose.

"To find what's been buried," I called back without turning. The door swung open, a sliver of daylight slicing into the solemnity of the room behind me.

Outside, the corridor was empty, the silence feeling strange in contrast to the clamor within. I took a deep breath, the chill of the tiles beneath my feet grounding me. The questions multiplied, each one a riddle wrapped in an enigma: who else knew, who else lied, and who else wanted Angela's story to end in darkness?

The click of my heels punctuated my resolve as I strode down the hallway, determination etched into every line of my frame. The hunt was on, and I was the hunter. This was far from over, and I would claw at the secrets until they bled truth.

My hand brushed against the phone in my pocket—Matt, Angel, the kids—they were my anchor, my reason to right wrongs. But for now, the pursuit consumed me.

The courthouse doors closed behind me with a resolute thud, a full stop to one chapter, and the sharp intake of breath before another.

"It's not over yet," I whispered to no one in particular. And with that, I stepped into the daylight, the weight of the unknown heavy on my shoulders but the fire of truth burning brighter within.

Chapter 25

St. Augustine's humid breeze crept in through a cracked window, wrapping around me like an omen. Later that same night, I sat on the edge of the Airbnb's couch, my skin prickling with the eerie sensation of unseen eyes boring into my back. My hand paused mid-air, the spoonful of ice cream forgotten as I scanned the darkening street outside. The lampposts cast long shadows, and for a fleeting second, I was sure one shifted against the rhythm of the swaying palms.

"Stop it, Eva Rae," I muttered to myself, dismissing the paranoia and returning to the ice cream I had allowed myself as a reward for my victory. Cases sometimes got under my skin and made me jump at my own shadow. But this was different—instinct honed from years in the field scratched at my consciousness, warning me not to ignore the feeling.

The sudden crash of the door slamming open shattered the evening's calm, and my heart catapulted into my throat. Detective Larson barreled into the room, his bulky frame filling the space with oppressive energy. His eyes, dark as the night engulfing us, glinted with a fury that rooted me to the spot.

"Thomas!" he barked, his voice a guttural growl.

I set the ice cream aside, standing to face him, my pulse racing yet my voice steady. "What's going on here, Larson?"

"Cut the crap!" He advanced one step, then another, closing the gap between us. His hands were clenched, knuckles white—a tempest barely contained. "You've ruined my life, my career! Go back to where you came from or—"

"Or what?" I shot back, meeting his glare head-on. Fear clawed at my insides, but I pushed it down, standing my ground. "You'll do what, exactly?"

His breath was hot and heavy, reeking of coffee and something darker, something sour. Alcohol. He had been drinking. We were inches apart, a dangerous dance playing out in the dimly lit room. The walls seemed to close in, suffocating, as the detective's shadow loomed over me.

"I'm not playing games, Thomas." His voice had dropped to a venomous hiss. "This is your last warning."

My hand twitched toward my phone, the urge to call for backup rising like bile. But I needed more than just my gut telling me Larson was dirty. I needed proof, something solid. And if he was willing to storm in here like a raging bull, who knew what else he was capable of?

"Warning heard," I said coolly, locking eyes with him. "Now, get out."

He studied me for a moment, the storm in his eyes swirling with conflict. His eyes narrowed, a dangerous glint surfacing as I remained immovable, an oak amidst his storm.

"Why are you so eager to get rid of me? What are you afraid will come to light?" I asked.

"Me? Afraid?" He scoffed, the sound sharp as shattered glass. "You're the interloper here, Thomas. Poking around where you don't belong."

"Because there's something wrong with this case," I persisted, my voice steady as a heartbeat despite the pounding in my chest. "There was a reason Carol lied, wasn't there?"

Larson's face contorted, a mask of fury replacing any pretense of professionalism. "Are you accusing me of something?" he spat, his words laced with poison.

"Are you telling me I shouldn't be?" I countered, keeping my tone level though my insides roiled with tension.

That was the spark that lit his fuse. In a flash, he was upon me, his hand snaking out, fingers like steel as they clamped around my collar. He shoved me, my back slamming against the wall with a thud that rattled my bones. His breath scorched my face, each word a serrated edge cutting through the air.

"Listen, you meddling little—"

"Detective," I gasped, struggling to maintain clarity as fear clawed its way up my throat. "This isn't the way."

"Shut it!" The pressure on my collar tightened, his grip unforgiving. "You've been a thorn in my side since you arrived, and I'm done playing nice."

"Assaulting an FBI agent," I managed to choke out, "isn't playing at all."

"Who's going to believe you?" His snarl was right in my ear, his threat unmistakable. "I'll make sure you never interfere again."

I felt the cold press of the wall through my shirt, the hard reality of my situation setting in. This man was desperate, dangerous—a cornered animal with nothing to lose. His eyes, mere slits of unbridled rage, told me everything I needed to know. If I didn't act or find some way out, my story would end here, in this nondescript room, far from those I loved.

"Think about what you're doing," I tried, my voice barely more than a whisper, but every syllable was a defiance, a refusal to succumb to the darkness encroaching on the edges of my vision. "Is it worth it, Larson? Is it really worth your badge, your honor?"

"Shut up!" The violence in his shout shook me to the core. I stared into the abyss of his fury, knowing I was dangling over the precipice by nothing more than his wavering self-control.

"Your call," I breathed, the words slipping out like a prayer, hoping against hope that somewhere within this broken man, a shred of decency remained.

The air hitched in my throat, the world narrowing to the brute force of his grip on my collar. Instincts honed through years in the field surged… a split-second glance at his exposed torso.

Now.

"Ugh!" My foot shot out, connecting with his abdomen. He grunted, the shock loosening his hands for that critical heartbeat.

"Damn you, Eva Rae!" he cursed, recoiling.

I twisted free, stumbling back. Adrenaline surged. Focus. I dove for my phone, skidding across the laminate floor.

"911, what's your emergency?"

"Detective Larson… he's here," I panted, "He attacked me. I need police."

"Stay on the line, ma'am. Officers are on their way."

"Fast, please," I managed, eyeing him, wary of another charge. It came seconds later. But not the way I had thought it would. I pressed record on my phone.

Larson's shadow stretched across the floor like a stain. He bolted for the door, but I was quicker, my body propelled by a cocktail of fear and fury. I intercepted him, blocking the doorway with an outstretched arm.

"Move," he hissed, eyes darting.

"Not a chance," I replied, voice steady despite the drumming of my heart.

Outside, sirens wailed their approach, the sound growing louder, more insistent. Panic flickered across Larson's face, his facade crumbling.

"Damn you, Eva Rae," he spat. "You don't understand. I had to stop her—Carol. She was going to ruin everything."

"By telling the truth?" I edged closer, cornering him. "By admitting she had lied? A lie you told her to tell?"

"Truth?" A bitter laugh escaped him. "She loved Will. Obsessed. When he rejected her after his wife died, she wanted revenge. It was perfect until you showed up. Carol got scared and said she'd confess to the lie. I couldn't allow that."

"Couldn't allow justice?" I pressed.

"Justice?" Larson sneered. "I made sure justice was done! Until you ruined it all. Will killed his wife, and I knew it. But the evidence… it was never enough. I had to ensure it."

"By telling a witness to tell a lie? By killing Carol because she wanted to tell the truth? By framing an innocent man?" My voice cracked like a whip.

"Will is not innocent!" His roar filled the room, but the nearing sirens swallowed his protest.

"Then why tamper with evidence, Larson? Why frame me?"

"Because you were close, too damn close. You always are." Desperation laced his words. "I needed to silence

Carol and you and was hoping to get you to go down for her murder. You were ruining my case against Will. He was going to go free. And he did, damn it. Because of you!"

"Then, you confess?" I needed him to say it. "You murdered Carol Rudolph?"

"Confess?" He laughed again, hollow. "Sure, I confess. I got rid of her before she could tell anyone. Just like I'll get rid of you. Happy now?"

"Ecstatic," I muttered, the sirens a crescendo outside.

My thumb hovered over the record button on my phone, my breath suspended. Shock grappled with instinct as Larson's confession twisted in the charged air. I pressed down, a silent click anchoring his words to memory—digital proof of his monstrous betrayal.

The wail of sirens surged, their urgency slicing through the tension. Blue and red lights danced across the walls, an eerie prelude to the reckoning that awaited. Larson's eyes flicked toward the window, then back at me, cornered prey in a trap of his own making.

"Damn you!" His voice was a thunderclap as officers burst through the door.

"Police! Hands up!" they barked in unison.

Larson raised his hands but hurled his fury at me. "This is your fault, Eva Rae!"

"Turn around!" An officer stepped forward, cuffing him with a cold click of finality.

"You ruined me!" He thrashed against the grip of law, spit flying. "If you hadn't stuck your nose where it didn't belong, we'd have him behind bars by now. You think you're so clean? You're a meddler, a—"

"Save it for your statement," I shot back, heart hammering yet steady.

"I'm taking you down with me—" His threat cut short as he stumbled, forced out by the officers.

"Watch your head," one said dryly, shoving Larson into the car outside.

I stood there, the echo of chaos fading, replaced with a deep silence that hummed with victory and loss. The detective's downfall was recorded on my phone, his curses lingering like ghosts.

The car door slammed shut, echoing down the quiet street. My hand was steady as I extended the phone to the officer still standing in the doorway.

"Here," I said, voice devoid of tremor. "Everything's on there. His confession."

He took it, nodding once, and turned away to listen. The screen's glow illuminated his face—a somber mask as the recorded venom spilled into the night.

"Good work, Agent Thomas," he muttered without looking up.

A shiver darted through me, not from the night air but from what lay within that device—the truth in digital form. My gaze fixed on Larson, now caged in the back seat of a squad car, his silhouette thrumming with silent rage.

"Thomas?" Another officer approached, notebook in hand. "We'll need your full statement."

"Of course." The words were mechanical, a reflex in the aftermath. I felt my neck and the bruises he was bound to have left.

"Take your time. We've got him." He gestured toward the car, where Larson's muffled shouts were barely discernible behind reinforced glass.

"Thank you," I whispered, my gratitude genuine but fatigued.

As they drove the car away, red lights painting the night, my legs buckled slightly, catching myself against the window frame. Relief surged like an adrenaline come-down, leaving my muscles weak and my mind frayed at the edges.

I watched the squad car disappear around the corner, the blare of the sirens fading into the distance. It was over—the threat, the lies, the confrontation—all distilled into the receding pulse of police lights.

"Agent Thomas?" The first officer handed back my phone, his expression unreadable. "I managed to copy the recording onto my computer."

"Call me Eva Rae," I corrected, reclaiming the device, its surface now oddly warm against my palm.

"Sure thing... Eva Rae." He offered a tight smile. "Get some rest. We'll be in touch."

"Rest," I echoed, knowing sleep would elude me, chased away by the shadows of what had transpired.

The officers left, their departure as brisk as their entrance, leaving me alone with the silence of the Airbnb, the memory of violence still clinging to the walls.

I sank into the worn armchair, the clamor of my heartbeat loud in my ears. The detective's confession reverberated through the hollows of my mind, each word a heavy stone in the fabric of the case. Carol's face flickered behind my eyelids—her life, her secrets, all buried under his ambition.

"Damn it," I muttered, rubbing my temples. My fingers trembled, betraying the adrenaline still coursing through me. I needed to calm down, to rest. But first, I had to let him know, let Matt know I was safe.

The phone felt alien in my hand as I dialed, the screen's glow glaring against the darkening room. One ring. Two. Then Matt's voice, a steady anchor in the chaos.

"Matt, it's me," I said, voice thick, a tear betraying my composure.

"Eva Rae? What's wrong?" His concern pierced through the line, immediate and sharp.

"I caught the detective," I managed to say. "But not until after he attacked me. He confessed to everything, though, so that's good."

"Jesus, Eva Rae...." He paused, the weight of his exhale traveling the distance between us. "Are you hurt?"

"Shaken. Not broken." A half-truth; my soul felt cracked at the edges.

"Thank God. I worry about you, you know that?" His voice softened, a balm to the night's violence.

"I'm coming home," I whispered, the words a promise, a plea for normalcy. "Tomorrow, as soon as I wake up."

"Good," he said, relief evident. "We all miss you. You've been gone too long."

"Miss you, too," I confessed, a sob catching in my throat.

"Stay safe tonight," he added. "Please."

"Always," I assured him, though we both knew the promise was as fragile as the silence around me.

Closing the call, I sat motionless, gathering the shards of courage scattered by the night's revelations. Tomorrow, I'd leave this place. For now, I held onto the threads of home, weaving them into armor against the darkness.

Chapter 26

THEN:

Laughter bubbled through the dining room of the elegant, candlelit home. Angela Jennings, with her bright blue eyes dancing merrily, shared a light-hearted story about their youngest's latest escapade in finger painting. The gathered friends, a medley of old college companions and newer acquaintances from the children's school, leaned in, captivated by her animated recounting.

"Pure Picasso," Angela concluded, her voice soft yet filled with mirth, eliciting a round of chuckles.

"Though I fear our walls are her preferred canvas," Will added, his warm tone carrying across the table, drawing a collective laugh.

"Thankfully, washable paints were invented," a friend interjected, raising his glass in mock toast.

Angela's gaze drifted, catching Will as he turned toward the woman beside him, a single woman new to their social circle. His hand lightly brushed hers as he passed the salt, their shoulders inching closer in the cozy atmosphere. Laughter spilled from his lips again, this time in a more intimate timbre, paired with a glance that lingered too long for Angela's comfort.

"Isn't that right, Will?" one of the guests called out, pulling him back into the wider conversation.

"Absolutely," he responded, but his eyes flickered back to the woman with a familiarity that twisted Angela's stomach into knots.

"More wine, Angela?" the hostess offered, breaking her fixation on the unfolding scene. She nodded, forcing a smile as her glass was refilled, its ruby contents swirling like her rising unease.

"Delicious," she murmured, the word tasting sour against her tongue.

"Angela?" Concern tinged Will's voice as he finally noticed her. "You okay?"

"Yes, why wouldn't I be? I'm fine, just… fine," she reassured, but her heart thundered a protest.

Memories of her mother's words echoed in her mind, a soothing mantra meant to dispel the shadows of doubt. After their last fight, she had come over and sat down with her, telling her she was acting crazy.

"You're creating stories, Angie." Her mother's voice was firm, unwavering. "Nothing is going on with Will. Nothing points to him cheating on you. You have to stop this madness. You will end up pushing him away."

She had to believe her mother was right. Trust was the bedrock upon which they'd built their life together. It was all in her head. It had to be.

"Excuse me," Angela whispered, her chair scraping softly as she stood. She avoided Will's questioning look, feeling the weight of the room's eyes as she slipped away. Her hands trembled slightly, not from the chill of the hallway but from the effort of keeping the storm inside her at bay.

The bathroom door clicked shut behind her. She leaned against the cool marble countertop, willing her reflection to show the strong, composed woman she needed to be. Trust him, she silently implored herself. You have to trust him.

Angela's fingers curled around the porcelain sink. She inhaled deeply, the cool air of the bathroom filling her lungs, steadying her. The scent of lavender soap mingled with her perfume, a calming presence.

Exhale.

Her reflection in the mirror no longer showed a woman on the edge but one determined to keep her composure.

"Trust him," she whispered to her image, a silent plea etched into her features. Another breath. "It's all in your head."

She straightened her blouse and smoothed down her skirt. Angela Jennings was not one to unravel, not here, not in front of friends. With one last glance, she opened the door and stepped back into the fray.

The buzz of conversation welcomed her return, a symphony of clinking glasses and shared laughter. Will's laughter rose above it all, too loud, too bright. Angela's gaze fixed on him and the woman whose hand now rested just a hair's breadth away from his on the linen-covered table.

"Everything okay?" The host's inquiry barely registered.

"Absolutely," Angela replied, her tone light, betraying nothing. She sat back down and reached for the bottle of Merlot, its dark promise grounding her. The liquid splashed into the glass, the sound sharp in her ears.

"Great party," she said, louder now, her voice finding strength. A half-smile played on her lips as she lifted the wine to them, savoring the bold flavor that failed to mask the bitterness creeping back into her throat.

Will's eyes met hers across the room, a flicker of something unspoken passing between them. But then he turned back, drawn into the orbit of the woman beside him once again.

The tightness in Angela's chest wound tighter, a coil ready to snap. She sipped again, the warmth of the wine spreading through her, a feeble armor against the chill of doubt.

Angela's hand trembled, the glass of Merlot a sudden weight. She watched, as if from outside herself, the scene unfolding. Laughter rippled from Will, an intimate sound shared with the woman beside him; her soft chuckles a melodic harmony to his baritone mirth. His hand now lay atop hers, their fingers inches from intertwinement.

"Excuse me," Angela murmured to no one in particular, her voice a ghost of its usual tenderness. She rose unnoticed, her chair scraping softly against the hardwood floor.

A step forward. Two steps. Her heart galloped, a frantic rhythm in her ears. The room seemed to stretch, time elongating as she bridged the space between betrayal and confrontation.

"Will," she said, louder now, but he didn't hear—or chose not to. His world had narrowed to the circle of light cast by the table's candles, illuminating the single woman who had become his solar system.

Angela's grip tightened. The stem snapped. Crimson spilled over her knuckles, that stood out on her pale skin. With a surge that funneled all her anger into a singular point of release, Angela hurled the contents of her glass.

Merlot arced through the air, a scarlet comet heading for a collision course with Will's face. Impact. Droplets scattered like shrapnel, some finding refuge on the white tablecloth, others on the faces of stunned guests.

Silence detonated in the aftermath. Silverware clattered to a stop. Conversations cut short. Eyes wide, mouths agape.

"Angela!" Will sputtered, wine dripping from his chin, his surprise giving way to indignation.

"Is this what we've become?" Angela's voice cracked the silence, sharp, carrying. "Am I just the ghost at your feast, Will?"

"Angela, what—?"

"No." She cut him off, stepping closer, her presence unyielding. "You're so busy charming every woman but your wife. Ignoring me, us, while you indulge in… in this!"

"Angie, please, it's not—" Will attempted to stand, to reach for her, but she recoiled.

"Save it!" She punctuated each word with pointed jabs of her finger. "I watch you. I see how you are with them. Laughing. Touching. Where is that man when he's with me?"

"Angela, let's talk about this," Will's tone softened, the plea clear in his eyes.

"Talk? Like you 'talk' to her?" Angela swept her arm toward the woman, whose face had paled, caught in the crossfire.

"Angela, don't do this here," Will implored, but the levee had broken. "I'm sorry everyone…."

"Here is exactly where we do this, Will! Because it's always here, among them, that I lose you!" Her voice swelled with a mix of sorrow and fury.

"Angie, you're overreacting," Will tried to reason, his

anger simmering beneath the surface. "Am I not allowed to talk to anyone but you?"

"Overreacting?" Angela laughed, a harsh sound. "No, this is me reacting, Will. This is me tired of being invisible."

Angela stood, breaths coming fast, the taste of bile and Merlot in her mouth. She stared at the wreckage before her—a nice dinner turned battlefield—and knew there was no retreat, only the grim march forward.

A plate shattered against the wall, a hair's breadth from Will's head.

"Angela, stop!" he shouted as another missile—this time, a fork—narrowly missed him.

"Shut up!" Angela's voice was a whip-crack in the dining room, her usually gentle blue eyes ablaze with an incendiary rage that belied her nurturing nature.

"Angie, please," Will's plea drowned under the clatter of silverware raining down on him.

"Please? Please?" Each word was punctuated by the thud of objects hitting the walls, the floor, and the table. "You never begged when you were ignoring me!"

"Angie, look at me. Look at me!" Will stood firm, arms raised defensively, trying to bridge the chasm of fury between them.

She lunged, hands clawing. Instinctively, he caught her wrists, pulling her into his chest, absorbing the kinetic wrath into his own body. "This is not you," he whispered, breath hot on her ear.

"Let go! You don't know me!" Her struggles were frantic and desperate, but slowly, the fire dimmed, choked out by sobs that racked her frame.

"I'm here, Angie. I'm not having an affair, I swear." His words wrapped around her like a blanket, soft and insistent.

"Then why?" she gasped, her voice muffled against his shirt. "Why do you push me away?" The vulnerability coiled within her, a wounded animal caged by its own despair.

"Angie, I'm not," Will's voice cracked, the lie of omission heavy on his tongue. He held her tighter, willing his heartbeat to steady hers. "I'm right here."

"Here," she echoed, the word hollow. "But not with me. Never with me."

"Always with you." He tilted her chin up, forcing her to meet his gaze, to see the truth—or at least the semblance of it—shining back at her.

"I wanna go home."

Angela ripped herself from Will's grasp, the fabric of his shirt still clutched in her trembling fingers. She staggered back, the image of their entwined shadows on the wall imprinting itself into her memory like a dark omen. Without a word, she turned, the echoes of her heels against the hardwood floor punctuating her departure. She ran to the car and got in, then waited for Will to join her. They drove home in silence.

The living room lay ahead, drenched in the soft glow of the evening light filtering through half-drawn curtains. Angela collapsed onto the couch, the cushions embracing her fall, while Will paid the babysitter and then went up to the bedroom without uttering a word to her. Her hands sought the familiar comfort of the throw pillows—tools of domestic bliss now smothered by the weight of her crumbling trust.

She lay there, her body a sprawl of abandonment, staring at the ceiling where the chandelier's crystals cast a mosaic of broken light across the plaster. Anger seethed within her, hot and acrid, gnawing at the edges of her composure.

"Perfect," she murmured to the empty room, the word a bitter twist on her lips. Their friends' laughter and wine glasses clinking now seemed distant memories. Betrayal, an unseen guest at the dinner party, had claimed its seat at the table.

Her thoughts spiraled with the ferocity of a storm. Every smile he had given that woman, each touch of his hand on her back—a tally of transgressions real or imagined. Angela's mind raced, replaying the evening's events, dissecting every gesture, every glance. In the quiet aftermath, doubt crept in, whispering sinister tales to her heart.

"Is there more?" she whispered into the dimming light, tracing patterns on the fabric of the couch as if it could yield answers. Her gaze settled on a photo of them on the mantelpiece, captured in a moment of genuine joy. How had they come to this—a tableau of affection now tinged with the hue of suspicion?

"It can't be just me."

Her voice cracked, the sound alien in the silence. She drew her knees to her chest, wrapping her arms around herself—a solitary attempt at self-preservation amidst the onslaught of uncertainty.

"There must be more to it…," she repeated, her voice trailing off as she sunk deeper into the couch's embrace, her sanctuary in the tempest of her emotions. The house, once filled with the melody of their life together, now resounded with the dissonance of unanswered questions.

Angela's chest heaved, each breath a battle against the swell of emotions that threatened to consume her. The soft fabric of the couch cradled her weary body as she lay there, a silent sentinel in the darkness that now filled the room. Her eyes, once bright with warmth and kindness, flickered in the gloom—haunted.

"Trust," she whispered to the shadows, the word a

hollow promise in the empty space. She searched for it, clawed for the certainty that love was meant to bring. But trust was a specter, slipping through her fingers like mist.

She shifted, restless, the elegant lines of her form etched with tension. Her fingers curled into the throw pillow, gripping it like a lifeline as her mind raced—a relentless tide of doubts and fears. What secrets did Will harbor behind those easy smiles? Was their life together just a well-crafted facade?

"I deserve answers," she murmured, the word less a demand now, more a plea to the universe. She wanted—no, needed—the truth, even if it shattered the fragile peace of ignorance.

Am I just losing my mind? Is my mom right?

But the weight of the night, the strain of the earlier confrontation, bore down on her. With her eyelids as heavy as lead, she fought against the pull of sleep, her resolve waning. Angela's breaths grew shallower, steadier, a reluctant surrender to exhaustion.

"Tomorrow," she resolved, a whispered vow carried off by slumber. "I'll find out. I'm no fool, Will Jennings. I will not let you make a fool of me."

And with that final thought lingering in the stillness, Angela slipped into a troubled sleep. Her form, a graceful silhouette cast in moonlight, breathed slowly, deeply—yet her brow furrowed with the ghosts of doubt that haunted her dreams.

Chapter 27

I zipped the suitcase with a sharp tug, the finality of the motion not quite matching the churn of doubt in my gut. Something was amiss—a piece of this twisted puzzle still eluded me.

"Let it go, Eva Rae," I muttered to myself, my fingers trembling as they clasped the suitcase handle. "Your family is waiting for you."

The house echoed with the hollowness of my departure, each step toward the front door amplifying the uncertainty that clawed at the back of my mind. I heaved the suitcase into the trunk, the thunk resonating like a gavel on judgment day. My hands swept over the pockets of my jeans, confirming keys, phone, and the ever-present sense of duty.

I slid behind the wheel, the leather of the driver's seat embracing me like an old friend. The engine roared to life, insistent and ready. I cast a last glance at the rearview mirror—the Airbnb shrinking away—and then, nothing but the road ahead.

The highway unfolded like a gray ribbon beneath a sky

heavy with unspoken secrets. Cars blurred past, their drivers unknowing of the storm brewing within me. With every mile marker I passed, determination sunk its teeth deeper into my resolve.

"You gotta let it go, Eva Rae," I whispered to the open air, foot pressing harder against the accelerator.

But I couldn't. Of course, I couldn't. It kept nagging at me, pulling me. My foot hesitated on the pedal; my breath hitched.

"Dammit," I exhaled, wishing I just wouldn't care so much. But I did, and that was my downfall.

I had to go back. I could never live with myself if I didn't. I simply couldn't leave an unsolved mystery behind.

The wheel jerked in my hands, tires squealing objections—a quick turn toward an exit carved into the asphalt like a desperate plea. I returned to I95 in the opposite direction.

Going back.

My heart thudded, the engine growled, hungry for truth, while my fingers drummed on the steering wheel. Doubt was a bitter taste at the back of my throat.

"You need to find the truth." The words tumbled out, unbidden. A mantra. "Before you can go back. Before you'll be able to let this case go."

The familiar turns loomed up, somber and foreboding. My car, an extension of will and fear, hurtled toward the house where Angela's life had spilled out over polished hardwood.

Each mile devoured brought me closer to the maw of revelation. The house stood sentinel, windows like vacant eyes. I parked with a screech, heart a drumroll against my ribs.

This was it—the dive back into the abyss.

"Show me," I breathed, hand finding the grip of my gun with practiced ease. "Show me what I missed."

GRAVEL CRUNCHED underfoot as I killed the engine and swung the door wide. The house loomed, a silent sentinel to secrets and lies. My sneakers hit the pavement, each step deliberate, echoing in the stillness that hugged the crime scene. No yellow tape fluttered in the breeze anymore; it had been three years, and the world seemed oblivious to the horror that had unfolded within these walls.

I rang the doorbell and then waited. There was no car in the driveway and no lights spilling from inside. When no answer came, I looked through the windows but saw nothing but vacant rooms inside.

I knocked.

"Will?" My voice sliced through the silence, hopeful yet wary. I listened, heartbeat drumming in my ears. Nothing.

I walked to the back and grabbed the sliding door that was still left unlocked. I walked inside.

"Will? It's FBI Agent Thomas. I need to talk to you. Are you home?"

The air felt stagnant, heavy with the absence of life. The void answered back—no footsteps, no breaths, just the whisper of dust settling into the grooves of time-worn floorboards. It didn't look like Will had been back here after being released. Everything looked just like when I was here last.

"Okay," I muttered, steeling myself. Adrenaline surged, visceral and sharp. "Let's take a look."

I stepped over the threshold, the weight of the unseen pressing close. It was as though the house had swallowed Angela whole, erasing her existence with a gulp of shadows and silence. But I was here to make it spit out the truth, however long it had been biding its time in the darkness.

I moved swiftly, my eyes raking over the mundane details of a life interrupted—of Will staying there for three years before his arrest. Three years after his wife had died in this very place. How did you do that? How did you cope with that? I once lost a dog very suddenly when I was younger, and I could barely be in my own apartment after that. But Will had lived here for three whole years. And then he had been arrested. One morning a couple of months ago, they had come for him, and no one had lived here since. I noticed the scatter of magazines on the coffee table, a half-empty mug of cold coffee crowning its ceramic surface.

The stairs loomed before me, wooden and unassuming. I could almost see her there—Angela, poised for a descent she'd never complete. The banister seemed to shiver with the ghost of her touch. My gaze crawled upward, tracing the path of her fall, and I shook the image from my mind.

Room by room, I scoured, flipping cushions and rifling through drawers—an intruder searching for the jagged piece of this puzzle. But each space yielded nothing, pristine to an unsettling degree. The kids had gone to live with their grandmother when their mother died. Yet their rooms still stood the same—like mausoleums over a time lost. The stairs leading me back down had been cleaned; you couldn't see the blood that was in the pictures in the case files anymore. The handprint on the railing was gone, too. It was like it had never happened.

Yet it had. And it creeped me out as I walked down the stairs, grabbing the railing as if I was afraid to suffer the same fate.

What made her fall? Was she drunk? On drugs?

The case files told me she usually had great balance.

She had even been a ballerina as a child. But the toxicology report also told me that she had no drugs in her system.

Could it be just an accident? Was I wrong about my strange feeling that it wasn't?

Something caught my eye: the door leading to the screened-in back porch.

I opened the sliding door and stepped out. The screen was ripped in places, and the area mainly served as a place for them to store their patio furniture.

"Stay sharp; look for anything abnormal," I murmured to myself.

And just like that, something in the corner caught my eye.

"Hello, what have we here?" The words were a whisper, a ghost's breath.

Moving closer, the porch surrendered its prize.

"What on earth…?"

The revelation was sharp, a shard of glass in my mind. This changed everything. The narrative, the suspect, the motive—they were all intertwined in this macabre story.

I swallowed hard, the taste of betrayal bitter on my tongue. Trust, once broken, turned the world into an alien landscape. Here, beneath the earth, surrounded by whispers of the past, I stood on the precipice of a staggering truth.

And it was making my blood run cold.

Chapter 28

My heart hammered against my ribs, thudding with a sense of urgency and fear as I slammed the heavy car door shut behind me. The sound echoed through the deserted driveway, a sharp contrast to the eerie silence of the darkened house in front of me.

With trembling hands, I fumbled for the keys and inserted them into the ignition, the familiar roar of the engine providing a comforting sense of control in this chaotic moment. My grip tightened on the worn steering wheel as I took deep, shaky breaths, trying to calm the coiling dread in my stomach. Every nerve was on edge as I prepared to make my escape from this place filled with grim revelations and haunting memories.

"Drive," I muttered to myself, slamming my foot onto the gas pedal with fierce determination.

The tires screeched against the asphalt, their grip biting into the ground like a cornered animal fighting for survival. Despite my desperate attempts to outrun it, I could still feel the residue of terror clinging to my skin like an invisible shroud that refused to let go.

"You have to follow this through, Eva Rae," I commanded myself, trying to drown out the chaos swirling in my mind. "You can't just sit back and let this killer, this cold-blooded murderer get away with it. Not on your watch!"

The implications of what I had uncovered unfurled before me like some grotesque tapestry, each thread woven from lies and betrayal. How could I have been so blind? As someone who constantly played with trust as part of my job, I should have known better than to gamble on those who were not worthy of it. But I had taken that risk and lost—drastically so.

"Never again," I whispered vehemently to the empty seat beside me.

A red traffic light loomed ahead, demanding a halt that I simply could not afford at this critical moment. Glancing left and right for any signs of life or movement—but finding none amidst the quiet hum—I tightened my grip on the steering wheel even further, steeling myself for what was about to come.

"Go."

I barreled through the intersection without hesitation, paying no heed to the red light glowing impotently in my rearview mirror. There was no turning back now, not when every second counted and every choice I made could be a matter of life or death.

"Damn it!" The curse erupted from me involuntarily as the full realization hit me—the evidence, the truth, it was all on me now. The killer thought they had covered their tracks so well, but they had underestimated one short, chubby redhead with a tenacity for digging deep into the darkest corners of any case.

"Matt... I know you want me home, but I have to finish this. I just hope you'll understand."

Saying his name made me feel awful. I was supposed to come home to them today. I had promised them. Once again, I would be neglecting my family, choosing a case over them.

But how could I go home now?

That's not who I am, and you know it, Matt.

I stared at my phone, wondering if I should call and tell him, but decided against it. He would be mad and try and talk me out of it. It was one more burden I couldn't have on my shoulders. Not now. Not today. I would have to act now and apologize later. It was simply the way it had to be.

The road stretched before me like a murky path shrouded in uncertainty, but I would follow it regardless. I was driven by an unbreakable love for my children and a burning need to expose the rot at the core of this case that threatened to tear apart everything I held dear.

Chapter 29

THEN:

Angela's grip tightened on the shopping cart handle, a single tomato rolling from its perch onto the tile floor. She barely glanced at it. The aisles blurred as she pushed through her grocery list with robotic efficiency, her mind churning. The small receipt she had found that morning was on her mind. It was tucked away in Will's jacket—too casual, too careless. It revealed a dinner for two when he should have been working late.

"Paper or plastic?" the cashier's words cut through her reverie.

"Plastic," Angela snapped, quicker than intended. Her apology was a murmured afterthought. She looked for her wallet in her purse, then realized she had forgotten it at home.

"I'm sorry, she said. "I seem to have forgotten…."

"It's okay," the cashier said. "We'll keep it here, and you can come back and get your groceries."

"I won't be long," she said. "I don't live far away."

She abandoned the cart without the usual bags in hand, the automatic doors shuddering behind her. The drive home was a blur, her thoughts a louder companion than the radio's chatter. Suspicion gnawed at her, a relentless pest. She was supposed to go to lunch before grocery shopping, but Sam had canceled at the last minute. She was coming home early. It would give her more time to prepare the meal for tonight. She was making something special, Will's favorite.

Roast and potatoes with gravy.

The turn into the driveway felt like crossing a threshold. Her pulse quickened; the steering wheel became slick under her palms. The car rolled to a stop, gravel crunching a finality that echoed in her chest.

Something was wrong. There was a car in the driveway that wasn't supposed to be there. Her heart dropped when she saw it.

"Keep it together," she whispered.

Her breaths came fast, uneven. A neighbor waved. Angela managed a half-hearted smile before she turned, the weight of her discovery anchoring her to the spot for a heartbeat too long.

"Stay calm, it's probably nothing. Don't get in your head; you know how you get," she urged herself, stepping out of the car and into the unknown that was her own front yard. Her resolve deepened with every stride toward the house. She couldn't lose her cool. She couldn't jump to conclusions again. Her therapist had taught her how to handle her emotions when they got the better of her. Breathing techniques. Thinking of something pleasant, and don't keep swirling around the same old thoughts of doom and betrayal.

So, she breathed. She took deep, long breaths and told

herself it was nothing. Everything was fine. Of course, it was.

Each step up the pathway felt charged, a deliberate march toward impending doom. She did her best not to make it feel that way. She told herself it was her who was wrong. She was the crazy one.

Her fingers danced a frenzied ballet around her keyring, keys jangling in discordance with her racing heart. The silver of the house key caught the afternoon light, a mocking glint before it slipped into the lock. She willed her hands steady, cursing the tremor that betrayed her inner tumult.

"Come on," she muttered, teeth gritted.

The lock yielded, and Angela shouldered the door open, stepping across the threshold into a silent void.

The stillness greeted Angela like an accusation. She paused to listen, the hum of the refrigerator piercing the quiet.

"It's very quiet," she whispered.

Angela's steps were soundless on the plush carpet as she moved through the living room. Her gaze cut sharp angles around the space, over the mantle where family portraits stood sentinel, to the corners where shadows gathered like conspirators.

Nothing was out of place, yet everything felt amiss. A cushion on the sofa sat too perfectly fluffed as if to say, "I've been touched." The very air seemed to hold its breath, charged with the unsaid, unseen.

Angela's hands grazed the back of the couch, her fingers tracing the fabric, searching for warmth left behind by another. Her pulse thrummed in her ears, a rhythm trying to sync with the truth that lay just beyond reach.

"Show me," she commanded the silence, her voice a mere thread of sound.

A blazer. And it wasn't Will's. It was a woman's. It was draped casually over the arm of the couch. Angela's breath caught—a silent gasp that clawed at her throat. The fabric was unfamiliar, the color too bold for her taste. It lay there, a flag of conquest, an emblem of betrayal.

"Whose is this?" Her voice barely broke the hush, a ghostly whisper to herself.

The air turned colder, or so it seemed to Angela, as she clutched her arms around her chest. She could feel the texture of the jacket in her mind, coarse and intrusive. The very sight of it—out of place, unwelcome—sent tremors down her spine.

Her heart hammered against her ribcage, each beat a drumroll of dread. She took a step, then another, her movements stiff and robotic. The echo of her footsteps filled the house, tapping against the hardwood floor as she approached the staircase.

"Keep going," she urged herself, each word punctuating her resolve.

Angela's hand trembled as it met the cool wood of the banister, her grip tightening with each step she ascended. The staircase seemed to stretch before her, an uphill battle toward a truth she wasn't sure she wanted to face. Step by step, she moved through the dim light, shadows playing tricks on her eyes.

"Stay calm," she muttered to herself, her voice a mere thread of sound in the vast canvas of silence enveloping the house.

She reached the landing, feet planted firmly on the upper floor. Heart racing, Angela paused, her breaths shallow and rapid. Her gaze swept across the hallway—left to right, right to left. Nothing seemed amiss, yet everything felt wrong.

"Show me everything," she whispered, almost a challenge to the universe or anyone who dared shatter her world. "I need to know."

The door to the bedroom was left ajar. Inside was a whisper of movement, the faintest shift in the air. Her eyes locked onto these subtle cues, each one a potential harbinger of the heartache lurking just beyond the threshold.

"Will?" Angela's call was a blade slicing the stillness, sharp and clear.

No answer came, only the heavy thud of her own heartbeat filling her ears. She edged forward, every sense heightened, anticipating the crack of her life splitting apart.

"It's probably nothing," she breathed, though relief eluded her. The house betrayed her with its normalcy, its quiet compliance in masking the chaos that surely simmered beneath.

"Where are you?" Her question hung in the air, unanswered, as she approached their bedroom door, the last sentinel guarding the secrets within.

Chapter 30

Rain lashed at the windshield, a relentless torrent that turned the mountain road into a blur of grays and murky shadows. I squinted past the wipers' frantic dance, gripping the steering wheel hard. My car's tires groaned against the slick asphalt, struggling for traction on the serpentine path that cut through dense forest and jagged stone.

Beneath me, the engine growled—a low rumble that fought against the howl of the wind. Water cascaded down in sheets, pooling in treacherous rivulets that threatened to sweep me off the precarious edge with every curve. Thunder rumbled, a distant drumbeat that echoed the pounding of my heart.

Headlights pierced the downpour, illuminating towering pines that swayed like drunken sentinels lining the road. Branches clawed at the darkening sky, their needles silhouetted like barbed wire against the storm's fury. Each flash of lightning cast the world in stark relief—a snapshot of wild beauty and danger frozen in time before plunging me back into near-blindness.

With each mile, the climb grew steeper, the turns tighter. My breath fogged the glass, mixing with the condensation that the heater struggled to dispel. I wiped at it impatiently, cursing under my breath. Every instinct screamed that this was madness, but I pressed on, fueled by the urgency gnawing at my gut.

At last, the cabin emerged from the maelstrom, its silhouette a darker smudge against the night. I eased off the gas, coaxing the car onto the narrow shoulder where gravel crunched beneath the tires. The vehicle shuddered to a stop, the engine ticking as it cooled.

I sat there for a heartbeat, the rain drumming a deafening tattoo on the roof. Water streamed down the windows, distorting the view of the cabin's porch, making it seem as if it were underwater. My hands trembled slightly—not from fear but from adrenaline sharpening my senses and honing my focus.

"Okay, Eva Rae," I muttered to myself, steeling my nerves. "Time to end this."

Pushing the car door open, I stepped out into the deluge. Rain plastered my hair to my face and soaked through my clothes in an instant, but I barely noticed the chill. My eyes flicked left and right, searching the shadows that loomed around the cabin.

The air was thick and heavy with the scent of wet earth and pine, and the sound of the storm seemed to swallow the world whole. Yet, beneath it all, there was something else—a tension that set my teeth on edge—a promise of confrontation, of truths about to be laid bare.

Slippery mud clung to my boots as I made my way up the path, a narrow ribbon of trampled grass that wound its way to the front of the cabin. Every step was a silent battle against the muck and the torrential downpour that tried to push me back. My fingers tightened around the grip of my gun, knuckles whitening with the effort to keep it steady.

The rain was relentless, pounding on my shoulders like an incessant drummer, urging haste and caution in equal measure. Water cascaded off my face, blurring my vision, but not enough to deter me from the task at hand. I kept close to the shadowed edge of the cabin, thankful for the obscurity provided by the storm.

I reached the window, my heart drumming in sync with the rain. Through the pane, distorted by rivulets of water, Will's figure was a smudge of complacency. He lounged in an armchair, the amber glow of a fire casting dancing shadows across his features. A smirk played on his lips as he toasted the air with his glass, the rich brown liquid catching the firelight.

"Enjoying yourself, are you?" I whispered, almost impressed by his nerve.

My pulse quickened—not from exertion but from the knowledge that every second counted. The rain continued its relentless assault, but inside, Will reveled in warmth and solitude, or so he believed. This was it—the confrontation I had been chasing. I wiped a hand over my face, brushing away the water and the doubt.

"Time's up, Will," I murmured, a promise to myself more than anyone else.

A silhouette caught my eye. My heart skipped into a gallop, pounding against my ribs as if trying to break free. Another figure, motionless, stood in the corner of the room.

I straightened up, wiping the wet from my face. The rain had soaked through my clothes, each droplet a cold reminder of reality. There was no turning back. A deep breath filled my lungs, mingling with the scent of pine and damp earth. It grounded me and sharpened my focus.

"It's time, Eva Rae," I whispered to myself. "You've got this."

I stepped back from the window, my sneakers leaving imprints on the muddy ground. Every cell in my body tensed, ready for what would come next. I approached the door, the weapon heavy and slick in my grip.

"I need answers," I demanded internally. "Now."

Hand hovering, I hesitated. Every scenario played out in rapid succession—ambush, deceit, the glint of a hidden weapon. Danger was a palpable taste in my mouth, metallic and sharp like the scent of lightning in the air.

Rain lashed, relentless. It muddled sound but did nothing to dampen the throb of adrenaline coursing through me. My fingers twitched, inches from wood that might as well have been a gate to the unknown. Still, I leaned closer, ear angled toward the sliver of space beneath the door.

Silence wasn't what I got.

Muffled laughter trickled through the gaps, a low hum of conversation barely discernible. Words lost to the downpour, their tone teased at normalcy. Was it a ruse? A casual chat over brandy had no place here, not with Angela's life snuffed out and justice hanging by a thread.

"Stay sharp," I muttered, a mantra against the unease.

The rain's rhythm shifted, a staccato on leaves, wind rising. It cloaked me, perhaps masking any giveaway sounds of my presence. Yet, there was something else—an undertone beneath nature's roar—a clink of glass, the shuffle of movement.

I straightened, instincts on overdrive, gun a cold weight against my palm. Showtime.

With purpose, I raised my hand to the worn wood surface of the cabin door. A deafening silence fell upon the clearing as if nature itself held its breath. Three sharp raps broke the quiet, the sound cutting through the storm like a verdict.

"Will!" My voice came out steel-clad, unwavering despite the tempest around me. "Open up. We need to talk."

Nothing.

My knuckles rapped hard against the door once more, three solid thuds that resonated with my pounding heart. Each knock was a drumbeat. There was no going back now. Whatever lay on the other side of that threshold was a mystery I was about to unravel.

"Will!" Louder this time, assertive, leaving no room for doubt or delay.

Rain battered the earth, a relentless drumming that drowned out all else. I stood motionless but for the rise and fall of my chest. The gun's weight was a constant in my hand as I scanned the tree line, searching for shadows that didn't belong.

Nothing.

My gaze returned to the door. Seconds stretched like hours.

The cabin door groaned, inching open. Hinges protested, voicing age and disuse. A sliver of light, then more, until Will filled the frame. His eyes widened, an eyebrow arching in silent question—or was it accusation?

"Will," I said, voice even, giving nothing away. "We need to talk."

The shadow beside Will moved—a person, half-shrouded in dimness. My eyes narrowed as I studied them, the shape of a shoulder, the tilt of a head.

Will's companion stepped forward, features emerging from obscurity. At that moment, I knew I hadn't been wrong.

And it just about broke my heart... for Angela.

"How could you, Will? How could you do this to her? She was right all along. And she knew, am I right? She caught you. She finally caught you and figured it all out."

Chapter 31

THEN:

Angela hesitated at the threshold of the bedroom before she stepped in.

The bedroom air hung heavy with an unfamiliar scent, sweet and floral, an invasion among the familiar. She swallowed hard. Her fingers brushed against the cool wall as if steadying herself against the swell of trepidation that rose within her chest like a tide.

Disheveled sheets clawed at the edges of the bed, tossed aside with careless abandon. The pattern of creases told a story Angela had never read—one written without her, in the ink of betrayal.

She approached the nightstand, each step measured, deliberate. There it was—the lipstick-stained glass of wine. Half-empty, its contents still, a mirror to the chaos churning inside her. Her hand hovered, trembling, above the curve of the stem, refraining from contact as though it might scald her skin.

"Will?" The word was a whisper, barely audible, a ghost of sound in the quiet room.

No answer came, but the room spoke volumes in its silence. The wine—red, bold, a favorite they shared on anniversaries—now stood as a bitter testament to her unraveling trust.

Her eyes, bright and searching, flitted across every surface, seeking evidence and lies. But there was only the glass, the perfume, the sheets—a triad of truth that bore into her, merciless and sharp.

"Damn you," she murmured, not loud enough for the world to hear but enough for her heart to feel.

Angela moved, each footfall a silent drumbeat marching her closer to the unbearable truth. The bathroom door stood ajar, a sliver of light cutting through the dimness. She could hear splashing water and muffled laughter—a symphony of the ordinary now grotesque in its implications.

She paused, breath held hostage by dread. Her hand found the door, pushing it wider with an assertiveness that belied her trembling limbs.

The sight unfurled before her like a nightmarish tapestry. Clothes, their clothes, littered the tile floor—his shirt, her dress—a breadcrumb trail of infidelity leading to the claw-foot tub.

And there, in the steaming water, entangled in an embrace as old as sin, were the two people Angela had trusted most: Will and her mother. Their skin flushed from warmth or wine, they were oblivious to the world crumbling outside their watery cocoon.

Angela's heart plummeted, shattering against the cold, hard reality beneath her feet. The air left the room, a vacuum where once was the promise of family and fidelity. Her eyes fixed on them, unblinking as if to sear the image into memory—a cruel reminder of the fragility of love and trust.

"Will?" It was barely a question, more an exhale of hopelessness, a single word carrying the weight of a thousand shattered dreams.

Time slowed, the only movement the lazy rise of steam whispering secrets to the indifferent walls.

His head jerked, eyes wide with shock, mouth agape. Their wet skin seemed to glisten with guilt under the harsh bathroom light. Her mother's eyes, a mirror of Angela's own, were clouded with something unreadable. The silence was deafening.

"Angela—" Will's voice broke, but she cut him off with a sharp raise of her hand. She stepped closer, the scattered clothes crunching beneath her feet.

"Explain," she demanded, her voice steady despite the chaos threatening to engulf her whole being.

He stuttered, no words forming, just the sound of betrayal sputtering from his lips. Her mother, too, was silent, her face a mask of remorse that couldn't hide the truth.

"Explain!" Angela repeated, louder now, her hands clenching into fists at her sides.

"Angie, I—" her mother started, but Angela recoiled as if struck.

"Silence," she hissed, her gaze locked onto Will. "I'm talking to my husband. How could you, Will?" The whisper tore from her throat, each word laced with an agony that turned her blood to ice.

Her chest heaved, heart pounding against her ribcage like a caged bird desperate for escape. The room spun, walls closing in, threatening to crush her where she stood.

"Angela, please," Will pleaded, reaching out to her from the bath.

But she stepped back, repulsion and disbelief etching lines across her face. His touch, once sought after, was now toxic—an anathema to every memory they had built together.

"Please," he said again, his voice a mere shadow of the conviction it once held.

"Save your breath," Angela replied, each word a dagger plunging into the soft underbelly of their marriage. Her world, once vibrant with love and trust, lay in ruins at her feet.

She turned on her heel, leaving them behind in the steam and the lies, her exit silent save for the pounding of her heart echoing in her ears.

Chapter 32

I barged into the cabin, rain streaming off my drenched clothes. The door slammed shut behind me with a clap that echoed through the wood-scented space.

"Hello, Diane."

My voice was steady despite the chill that clung to my bones.

Surprise flickered across her features. "Eva Rae? What are you doing here?"

Memories of this place rushed back—the laughter, the warmth, the sense of innocence now tainted by recent events.

"I remembered I came here as a child, with my mom, to visit you." I peeled off my jacket, water pooling on the floorboards. "I called my mother on my way here to ask if you still had the cabin in North Carolina. You did. I figured if I were running from a murder, this would be the place to go."

Will emerged from the shadows behind Diane, his presence like a cold draft seeping into the room. Their eyes met

—held—a silent conversation passing between them. Wordless, but I heard it loud and clear.

"Running from a murder?" Diane's attempt at nonchalance came off as strained, her smile too tight.

"Sounds about right," I said, watching them closely.

They shared another glance, fleeting but heavy with unsaid truths. Will opened his mouth and closed it, a frown creasing his forehead. Diane bit her lip, a move so subtle that anyone else might have missed it.

I locked eyes with Will, seeing the crack in his facade. They tried to mask their panic with platitudes, but I saw through the charade. They knew that I knew.

"Let's sit down," Diane suggested, gesturing toward the worn sofa with a hand that trembled just slightly. "You must be freezing."

"No, thanks." I stayed where I was, grounded, unyielding. "I prefer to stand."

Diane nodded. "Fair enough. So tell me. How did you find out?"

I stepped closer, my gaze unwavering. "The back patio of Will's house," I began, the words carrying the weight of irrefutable evidence. "It's amazing what you can find when you're not even looking. A letter here, a photo there, and suddenly, everything falls into place. You kept it all out of the digital world. While Angela was looking through your computer and your phone, you had it all hidden in the physical world. Pictures of the two of you together, from trips you went on and dinners you had, were taken with a Polaroid camera. I found some letters that Diane had written to you and delivered via old-fashioned mail. She made sure they were sent to the clinic, so Angela wouldn't see them. But you left no trail that way, and that was your goal. You tried to burn it all, didn't you? After she was dead, and the police were looking through your house. You wanted to get rid of it. I found it all in your firepit on the back patio. You set it on fire and thought it was all done. But it wasn't all gone. You forgot to check; you got sloppy. I managed to piece it together by what was left."

Diane's face paled, her mask of composure slipping. Will's jaw clenched, his eyes narrowing.

"Angela knew, didn't she?" My voice was steady; my accusation pointed like the tip of a blade. "She suspected an affair, but how could she imagine it was with her own mother?"

"Stop this," Diane whispered, her elegant facade crumbling as I laid bare their secret.

"Unbearable, wasn't it, Will?" I pressed on, relentless. "Trapped in a marriage, longing for her," I nodded toward Diane. "So you made a choice. Together."

Chapter 33

THEN:

Angela stormed into the bedroom, her heart pounding against her ribcage. Will followed her.

"Angela, I… I…."

"How could you do this to me? I… I gave you children. We were a family. You told me I was crazy, but you were having an affair all along. How could you do this to me? To your wife?"

Her voice broke, a tremor betraying the storm of emotions within as she faced Will across the room. The question hung heavy in the air, laced with betrayal. "And with my own mother?"

Will froze beside the bed, his face contorting as if he'd bitten into a bitter fruit. "Angela, I—" Guilt flashed across his features, quickly masked by a hardening jawline. "You've got it all wrong," he said, his voice climbing with each word. "It's not what you think. You're seeing things again. It's wrong, Angela."

"Wrong?" Angela's hands shook at her sides, fingers

curling into fists. Her blue eyes, usually reservoirs of warmth, now sparked with the hurt that seared through her composure. "Don't lie to me!"

"Believe what you want!" Will's attempt at a rebuttal came out strangled, caught between self-defense and the truth he couldn't seem to face. His stance widened as though bracing against an invisible force.

She stepped closer, the space between them electric with tension. "I deserve the truth."

"Truth?" Will spat out the word, a sneer creeping onto his lips. "You think you're so perfect, don't you? Always the martyr."

Her retort was sharp, a blade unsheathed. "I am your wife!"

"Sometimes, I wonder!"

Will's words cut through the air, jagged and raw. Each syllable dripped with a venom that seemed foreign coming from him.

"Is that how little we mean to you?" Angela's voice crescendoed, filling the room with the sound of a heart fracturing. She searched his face for the man she married but found only a stranger wearing Will's skin. "Me and the children?"

His stance shifted, a mixture of defiance and desperation. "It's always all about you. You never see it, do you? How you push people away."

"By loving them?" Her whisper was a wail wrapped in disbelief.

"By smothering them!" Will countered, his palms upturned as if presenting an obvious fact Angela had missed.

"Love is not suffocation," she said, steadying her voice with effort.

"Isn't it?" He raised an eyebrow, challenging her belief, her vision of their life together.

"Love is trust, Will." Angela's gaze didn't waver, even as her world did, crumbling around her. "Something you've just destroyed."

He exhaled and shook his head. Will's jaw clenched, his eyes darting away from her piercing blue gaze. "You wouldn't understand," he muttered, a thread of escape in his voice.

"Make me understand!" The plea was sharp, her insistence a tangible force in the room.

"Stop it, Angela!" He flung the words at her like stones.

"Stop what? Caring?" Her arms spread wide, a gesture of her bewildered heart.

"Twisting everything." Will's hands balled into fists at his sides.

"Nothing is twisted about betrayal!" She stepped forward, her spirit unyielding.

"Isn't there?" His laugh was hollow, cold as the void between them.

"Tell me why!" Angela reached for him, seeking something to hold onto in the chasm that had opened beneath her feet. "Why her of all the women in the world?"

"Enough!" Will's shout splintered the air. He lunged, his movements sudden and violent.

Angela recoiled but not fast enough. His fingers wrapped around her arm, vise-like, unforgiving. Her skin burned beneath his grasp.

"Let go," she gasped, the words barely escaping her constricted throat.

"Angela…." His breath was hot against her face, his grip unrelenting.

Panic surged through Angela's veins, primal and fierce. She twisted against the iron clamp of Will's fingers.

"Get off me!" Her cry was a shard of glass in the thick air, her breaths coming quick and ragged.

Will's hold didn't slacken, his eyes a tempest of emotions she could no longer read. She pushed against his chest, her muscles coiled with urgency. Every fiber in Angela's being screamed to be free, to escape the suffocating grip that threatened to snuff out her light.

"Angela, you're not listening—" His words splintered as she cut him off.

"Neither are you!" Her voice was a whip-crack, splitting the tension.

She shoved harder, the force of her push fueled by betrayal, fear, and the need to protect herself from the man she no longer recognized. Their dance was desperation and denial, a macabre ballet in the half-light of their bedroom where shadows clung to the walls like silent witnesses.

"Stop," he growled, but Angela heard only the call of survival.

"Never." The word was a bullet, fired with all the strength she had left.

Their bodies collided and recoiled, a violent rhythm that matched the pounding of Angela's heart. Every shove and twist echoed the love that had once bound them, now frayed and snapping like an overstressed rope.

"Let go," she panted, her will an unyielding force as she struggled to break the bonds of his faltering resolve.

Will's face contorted, a grotesque mask of fury twisting his features. His hands, once tender in their touch, were now weapons fueled by a dark desire he could not name. His breaths came ragged; each inhale was a battle, each exhale a storm.

"How long?" Angela spat. "How long has this been going on?"

She looked at her mother, who shook her head. "Weeks? Months?"

Her mom shook her head again.

"Y-years?"

"It started at the engagement party," she said, her voice barely a whisper.

Angela felt her heart drop. This couldn't be true. They had betrayed her for years? For her entire marriage? She had been right all along? They had both told her she was crazy—that she was making things up. But she had been right all along?

"I need to be alone. Please leave me alone," she said, addressing the two of them. "Diane? I want you to leave, and I never want to see you again."

Her mother nodded, then gathered her things and left. Will followed her out and closed the door behind them.

Angela was alone now, sitting on the bed staring at her hands, not knowing what to do next. She sat like that for hours, hearing the kids come home from school, hearing their dad make them dinner, and later put them to bed. Angela didn't move. She just sat there, listening to the sounds of life moving on.

At eleven p.m., Will came to the bedroom and turned on the lights.

"Are you just going to sit there?" he asked. "You don't even care that your children missed you? I told them you were sick and to leave you alone. I fed them and put them to bed all by myself."

"You want me to thank you for that? Give you a medal?" she hissed.

"Well, it wasn't a lie. You are really sick if you think anything was going on between your mother and me."

"You're telling me that what I saw wasn't real? That I'm making it up?" she asked, rising to her feet.

"Enough!" The word erupted from Will, guttural, edged with venom. "Just get out of here if that's what you want."

She nodded. "I think that is exactly what I want."

Without another word, Angela walked to the door and into the dark hallway. Will sprang after her, grabbed her shoulder as she reached the top of the staircase, and made her turn around.

"You're sick, do you know that?" he spat. "That's what I'll tell everyone. Who will they believe, huh? The well-esteemed pediatrician whom everyone in the community knows and loves? Or the crazy lady who attacks neighbors and her own husband at dinner parties? I have a pretty good guess which way they'll lean."

"You slept with my mother," she said, then laughed. It came off as manic, crazy even. "You sick, sick pervert."

Angela, her heart a thunderous drumbeat in her chest, felt the world tilt as Will's shove sent her spiraling into chaos. Time fractured into a series of snapshots: his hand releasing her arm, the sudden absence of his weight, the rush of cold air where warmth had been.

Her body, graceful even in panic, betrayed her. Limbs flailed, seeking purchase in the nothingness that greeted her. Fabric whispered against skin, a cruel imitation of intimacy as her clothes billowed around her in an unforgiving dance.

The staircase loomed, an unyielding specter. Gravity, merciless in its decree, pulled her down. She reached out, fingers grabbing for the banister, a lifeline just beyond her grasp. But then a second shove made her hand slip, and that was the end of it. The abyss claimed her, and soon, the darkness as she hit the bottom of the stairs.

Impact. Wood met flesh with a brutal kiss, the sound reverberating through the hollow spaces of the house. Pain bloomed, a cruel garden growing wild and unchecked.

But Angela Jennings, whose compassion painted her world in hues of love, lay still at the foot of the stairs, silence her only response.

The silence struck Will harder than any scream. His breath hitched, his eyes stretching wide as the truth crashed into him with more force than Angela's body had met the staircase moments before. Horror etched deep grooves in his face, a grotesque sculpture of regret.

"Angela?" The name, usually a tender murmur from his lips, was now a shard of glass in his throat.

Motionless, she lay. A crumpled form at odds with the vibrant woman who breathed life into every room she entered. Blonde hair fanned out, an eerie contrast to the dark wood beneath her. Angela's chest rose and fell with the faintest quiver, each shallow breath a whisper of the pain radiating through her, her fingers digging their nails into the wooden floors below.

"Angela!" His voice broke, splintering the stillness. No soft, soothing tone answered—no firm resolve to steady the spinning world.

Will stumbled forward, knees weak, the distance between them an abyss he had created. His hands trembled with dread. He ran down the stairs.

"Please," he begged to the quiet. "Please. I'm sorry. I'm so, so sorry."

But Angela, the heart of their home, remained silent, her bright blue eyes staring at him, blood running from the back of her head where she had collided with the large vase at the base of the stairs. Her strength, so often a quiet undercurrent, had been consumed by the violence of the fall.

"Angela, I…."

Words failed, guilt choking him, turning his plea into a strangled gasp.

The house, their sanctuary, stood witness to the tragedy, its walls closing in, suffocating. In the wake of his actions, Will found himself alone, unable to act or know what to do next.

And then there was something else. Panic.

It clawed at Will's insides, a feral thing desperate to escape. Her stillness screamed louder than any cry for help. His gaze darted over Angela's form, the angle of her limbs unnatural, chilling. Blood—a dark red against the soft hue of her blouse—began to bloom.

He should call for help, should be pressing his hands to wounds, should be doing something other than staying there, drowning in the rising tide of his own fear. But the phone felt a universe away, and his body refused to obey. He was a doctor. He knew what to do.

Yet he didn't.

Instead, Will backed away. Each step was a betrayal, his heel a gavel condemning him. The staircase loomed above, an escape route, a coward's path.

"Forgive me," he choked out, the words empty, futile.

He pivoted, the motion jarring, and took the stairs two at a time. His breath came in sharp bursts, punctuating the silence that had devoured any trace of the life they had built.

The bedroom door slammed shut behind him, the sound a punctuation mark to the end of Angela's quiet strength and their shared dreams. Alone now, with only his racing heartbeat for company, Will leaned against the cool wood, gasping for air, for absolution, for anything but the truth of what lay below.

Her absence was a void, pulling him toward an edge he could never return from.

Chapter 34

"You left her to die, Will. Tell me I'm wrong about this. I think she might even have been able to make it if you had called for help when it happened. There are scratch marks on the floor where she was lying that you weren't able to erase. She was still alive, wasn't she? You were so coldhearted that you went back to bed and waited until someone else found her. Your own son had to find his mother on the floor in a pool of blood. Imagine what that does to a young boy. How do you live with yourself?"

"Enough!" Will's voice boomed through the cabin, his desperation palpable.

"You pushed her," I declared, each word a nail in their coffin of lies. "You finally had enough, and you decided just to get rid of her so you could be with the woman you love. Didn't you?"

"Shut up!" Will roared, lunging toward me, driven by fear and guilt.

Diane reached out, her hands clawing at the air. "Please!"

My instincts flared, honed from years of rigorous

training and fieldwork. A twist of my hips, a pivot on the balls of my feet, and I evaded Will's outstretched arms, his fingers grazing the fabric of my soaked shirt. Diane swung next, her desperation giving strength to her blow, but it was graceless, untrained. I ducked and felt the whoosh of air as her hand passed over my head.

"My guess is that you wanted to wait until a few years after Angela's death to really be together. You didn't want your relationship to seem suspicious. And you almost made it. Three years had passed, and so far, no one suspected a thing. But then came Carol, the neighbor, and she ruined everything. When she told her lie, instigated by Detective Larson, fueled by her anger toward you for not wanting her, you ended up in jail. Where you both belonged. You two murdered her. Your own daughter, Diane."

"Stop!" Diane's plea was sharp, a knife-edge of panic. "Stop talking."

"Can't do that," I shot back, voice even, breath measured.

Will lunged at me again. The cabin's cramped space turned into a battleground of shadows and flickering light, every move calculated, every breath a measure of life or death. I feinted left and dodged right, putting precious inches between us. Will's heavy breathing filled the room, a bull snorting steam, ready to charge again. But I had my gun, and as I raised it, they finally backed off.

"Think about this!" I warned them, the agent in me still seeking resolution over violence. "It's not too late to surrender."

"Never," Will spat and lunged again.

I caught his wrist, twisted—hard—and heard the grunt of pain as he recoiled. Diane hesitated, torn between aiding Will and fleeing. I pushed Will back, not wanting to hurt him, then lifted the gun again. I grabbed my phone, wanting to call for help. I managed to dial 911, but in that moment I looked away, Diane was the one who made a fatal decision. She grabbed the fire poker and swung it at me. Pain shot through my head, and the fall to the wooden floors made me drop my gun. For a few seconds, all I saw were stars, and as I rose up on my arms, trying to steady myself, Diane was holding my gun, pointing it at me.

"Think of it," she said, addressed to Will. "She's the only one who knows. I bet she came all this way alone without telling anyone where she was going. I say we kill her now and bury her in the woods."

Will hesitated, then said, "They'll be able to trace her phone."

"You're right. We'll take it with us when we leave and drop it somewhere else, far away from here. They might track it to this place eventually, but no one knows we were even here, and we'll be in California by then."

"Okay," Will said with a nod. "Do it."

Diane pointed the gun at my head, then hesitated for a second. That was all I needed.

A surge of adrenaline propelled me forward. I bolted for the door, heart pounding. Will and Diane screamed behind me, and the gun went off, the bullet hitting the doorframe next to me.

It shocked me, yes, but I didn't stop.

The cold slap of rain hit my face as I burst outside, freedom just strides away. Behind me, I heard the crash of a chair hitting the floor, Diane's cursing, and Will's enraged shout. But I was already moving, sprinting down the muddy path, determined to end this, to get out of there alive.

Chapter 35

Rain pelted my face, and the world became a blur of gray and green as I pounded down the path. I couldn't get to the car since I had dropped my jacket in the cabin when falling, and the keys were in the pocket. I had to get away on foot—hide somewhere or find help. I could hear their voices as they tried to catch up with me.

My sneakers slipped in the mud, but I didn't slow down. Branches whipped at my face, stinging like accusations. I could hear Will's heavy footsteps sloshing through the muck behind me, Diane's breathless calls growing fainter.

"Stop her!" Diane bellowed, her voice carrying an edge of terror that only the guilty can muster.

I knew this terrain, the treacherous dips and deceptive turns. As a child, I'd conquered these woods playing hide-and-seek with ghostly shadows when my mom brought me to visit Diane. Now, the game was deadly serious.

"Give it up, Eva Rae!" Diane's plea sounded distant, almost lost in the roar of the storm.

"Sorry," I muttered to the wind, "can't do it."

A fallen log loomed ahead, slick with rain, a natural barrier I remembered well. I hurdled over it without breaking stride, hearing the thud of Will's body slamming into the obstacle. His curse sliced through the storm.

"Dammit, Eva Rae!"

Ahead was the narrow bridge over the creek, its planks treacherous with moss. I took it at a run, each step a gamble. Behind me, a shout of warning—too late. I heard the sound of splintering wood and a splash. Diane had missed her footing.

"Help!" Her voice was pitched high with panic, fighting to get back up. She managed to pull herself out of the river, and soon she was after me again.

"Keep going," I commanded myself, heart racing. I couldn't afford the distraction.

The path forked, and I veered left toward rocky ground where the trees grew dense. Roots snaked across the path, tripwires for the unwary. I danced between them, agile despite the urgency clawing at my chest.

"Rae!" The call came from above. Will had gained higher ground, trying to cut me off.

"Nice try," I gasped, banking sharply to the right, my wet hair plastered against my skin. The incline steepened. Loose stones rolled beneath my feet, but I kept my balance, always moving.

"God damn you, Eva Rae!" Will's voice cracked with desperation. He was close, too close.

I pushed harder, legs burning, lungs tight. A clearing opened up... the old tree house silhouetted against the stormy sky. Memories flashed—laughter, secrets shared in that wooden fortress. Not today. Today, it was a landmark for evasion.

"Going to need more than that," I panted.

"Where are you?" Will's confusion was palpable, his movements erratic.

"Over here," I lied, voice bouncing off trunks and leaves.

"Gotcha now!" he roared, deceived.

I doubled back, putting distance between us, letting the forest cloak my escape. The sound of pursuit grew distant, then faded altogether. For a moment, I allowed myself to breathe.

But only a moment.

As I continued, the ground suddenly gave way to open air, a sheer drop just feet from where I staggered to a halt. Rain slicked the cliff's edge, a treacherous sheen under the storm's rage. Behind me, Will's labored breaths merged with Diane's frantic whispers. I was trapped, cornered.

No more running.

"End of the line, Eva Rae," Will panted, his voice a low growl. "There's nowhere to go."

"Think, think," I muttered, my heart thundering in my chest. One chance.

"Give up," Diane called out, her tone deceptively soft. "You have nowhere to go."

I feigned defeat, shoulders slumping. "You're right."

"Smart girl," Will sneered, edging closer.

Diane stayed back, caution in her gaze. I turned slowly, facing them. My eyes flicked between their faces, reading the tension, the expectation. Then, my eyes dropped to my soaked shoes.

"Always loved this view," I said, stalling, buying precious seconds.

"Shut up!" Will snapped.

I edged back, feeling the void at my heels. A gust of wind whipped my hair across my face, stinging my eyes.

"Remember the old hiking trick?" I asked, a spark igniting within me.

"Trick?" Diane frowned, puzzled.

"Distraction." I lunged sideways, yanking a branch from the ground.

"Get her!" Will roared.

I swung the branch like a baton, connecting with his shin. He howled, collapsing forward as his foot slipped in the wet mud. Momentum took him, and he clawed at the air, panic flashing in his eyes.

"Will!" Diane shrieked, darting forward.

"Bad move." With the last of my strength, I kicked loose a rock into her path.

She stumbled, a cry escaping her lips as she faltered, reaching for something... anything. But there was nothing —only the void, the pull of gravity, relentless and final. Her blue eyes met mine, a silent plea, and then she was gone, following Will into the abyss.

The cliffside was suddenly silent, the storm's roar distant, like a bad dream fading at dawn. I peered over the edge, the darkness below swallowing everything, even the guilt gnawing at my conscience.

They'd chosen this end, not me.

I stood, heart hammering, the night air cold against my sweat-drenched clothes. The cliff had claimed them, their screams swallowed by the abyss. I could hardly believe it— gone. Just like that.

"Dammit," I muttered, my voice a ragged thing in the stillness. Images of Will and Diane spiraled through my mind, but I shoved them away. There was no time for remorse or what-ifs. I had to act to ensure their story ended here.

I tread lightly over the sodden leaves, each step a silent promise to those who had suffered. The night air, thick with the scent of wet earth, wrapped around me, a reminder of the raw vitality of life and its fragility.

"Never again," I muttered, my breath forming clouds that danced away into darkness. My mind replayed the evening's events—a macabre waltz of deceit and desperation. Trust shattered in the face of betrayal; it was a lesson hard learned.

A rustle in the underbrush snapped me to attention. Instincts honed by years in the field kicked in. I reached for the sidearm no longer there—it lay somewhere below, wherever Diane had ended her days.

The path ahead wound down toward the lights of civilization. As I walked, careful not to slip and fall, I could hear the distant hum of an approaching engine growing louder. My heart pounded, not from exertion but from a surge of gratefulness flooding my veins.

Ahead, blue and red lights flickered between the branches, signaling the arrival of help. They had gotten my call when I thought it hadn't gone through. I quickened my pace, my thoughts racing faster than my feet. Angel's face flashed in my mind, her innocence a beacon guiding me home. Matt, Olivia, Christine, and Alex—they were my anchors, my reasons to keep the fight alive.

"I'm coming home," I whispered to the rain, this time as an oath to them, to myself.

I emerged from the tree line, squinting against the glare of headlights. A deputy jogged toward me, his expression a mix of concern and respect. I showed him my badge.

"FBI Agent Thomas."

"Agent Thomas. You're bleeding from your head. Are you all right?" he asked, steadying me as I approached.

"Better now," I replied, my voice firm. "Let's get this scene secured. There's a story here that needs to be told right."

Epilogue

I pushed open the front door, the salty tang of Cocoa Beach air clinging to my skin. My red hair, tangled from the drive, fell in a messy cascade down my shoulders as I stepped across the threshold.

Home.

The word resonated within me, a soothing balm to the fatigue that had settled deep in my bones. The paramedics had cleaned my wound, and they had taken me in for a couple of stitches and observation, so I spent the night at the hospital before I could finally come home later the next day. Now, it was afternoon, and I had finally arrived where I truly belonged.

"Mommy!" The squeal pierced the stillness. Angel, her red curls a wild halo, barreled toward me, arms outstretched like tiny wings eager for flight. Her freckled face was a beacon of pure joy.

"Hey, sweetie," I managed, just as her small body crashed into mine. Embracing her, I drank in the scent of bubblegum shampoo and crayons—a reminder of innocent days spent coloring outside the lines.

"Mom!" Alex's voice, a blend of boyish excitement and emerging maturity, cut through the laughter. He skidded to a halt, soccer cleats scuffing the floorboards. His sandy blond hair was tousled, his green eyes alight with the thrill of the game he'd been playing moments before.

"Look at you, champ." I ruffled his hair, noting the determined set of that jaw—so much like mine. "Missed you."

"Missed you more," he said, his smile faltering for a moment, hinting at conversations we'd need to have. But not now. Not yet.

"Group hug," Angel commanded, tugging at my sleeve, her eyes wide with expectation.

"Of course," I obliged, dropping to one knee to envelop them both in my weary arms. We fit together, a puzzle completed once again. The room echoed with their giggles, and I thought maybe, just maybe, I could find a way to be both their protector and their mother.

"Promise you'll stay?" Alex's voice was a whisper against my ear, vulnerable yet fierce.

"Everything I do," I whispered back, "I do to come back to you." And at that moment, surrounded by the chaos and love of my youngest children, I believed it with every fiber of my being.

The moment stretched, fragile as a soap bubble, and then Matt was there. A shadow cut from the doorway, his silhouette broad and unyielding.

My heart stuttered. Gosh, he was handsome.

"Eva Rae." His voice held that edge—the one that could slice through steel or cradle you like a lullaby. Now, it was a blade. "You're back."

"Matt." I straightened, an apology teetering on my lips, but he was already closing the distance between us.

"Back," he repeated the word like a bullet. "After

another close call. Another 'last-minute lead.' Do you even know what your absence does to us?"

"Matt, I—"

"Promises, Eva Rae. You made them." He was standing too close, his breath a hot gust against my face. "You promised you'd come home. Back to safety. Back to us."

"And I did. I'm here now."

Matt scoffed. "Whoop-de-do. You couldn't even have called us to say you were heading to North Carolina instead of home?"

"You would have tried to talk me out of it."

"Darn right, I would. It was dangerous. You were almost killed. You didn't need to go all alone, being a hero, catching killers on your own. One of these days, you won't win. They'll get you, and where will that leave us?"

"I do everything I do for you, for my children. It's not just about catching killers. It's about making sure there's one less monster out there. To make a safer world for my children to grow up in."

"Monsters." His laugh was short and devoid of humor. "And what about the monsters here? The fears that keep these kids up at night? Fears that their mom won't make it home?"

"Everything I do is to protect them." My words were shards, sharp and desperate. "To protect our future."

"Protect?" The skepticism in his eyes stung. "Or escape into a world where the rules are clear—where you don't have to navigate bedtime stories and parent-teacher conferences?"

That stung.

"Matt, please." I reached out, fingers grazing his arm, feeling the coiled tension beneath his skin. "That's not fair.

This is not to avoid the chores of having children. You know why I do this."

"You want me to understand?" He shook off my touch, stepping back. "I try, Eva Rae. God knows I try. But your choices are questionable. You act irrationally, recklessly. And it scares me."

His voice cracked, a fissure in the bedrock of his resolve. "And of course, I do understand, heck, I'm a cop myself. But I got hurt in the line of duty, and so can you. Understanding your motives for doing what you do doesn't mean I can stand by while you put yourself in the crosshairs."

"Crosshairs," I echoed as if tasting the word for the first time. It felt bitter. Dangerous.

"Listen to me." He leaned in as if imparting a secret. "I need you here, whole and alive. They need you. Can you promise me that?"

"Matt—" But the plea lodged in my throat. There were no guarantees in my line of work, no certainties except the knowledge that evil didn't clock out at five.

"Can you?" The demand hung between us, an ultimatum without words.

My silence was answer enough.

I swallowed the lump that had wedged itself stubbornly in my throat. "Matt, I'm sorry." My voice was a whisper, laced with the weight of days spent chasing shadows while home faded to a mere memory.

He stood rigid, the lines on his face etched with worry and sleepless nights. The silence between us stretched too thin, threatening to snap.

"I missed you," I said.

"Missed isn't enough, Eva Rae." His voice boomed suddenly in the quiet room. "Not when every phone call could be the last."

"Balance," I started, but the word felt foreign, like something borrowed and never fully understood. "I'll find it. For us."

"Balance?" Matt scoffed, a harsh laugh that didn't reach his eyes. "How do you balance life and death, Eva Rae?"

His gaze bore into me, searching for an answer I didn't have.

"Tell me you'll stay safe," he demanded, his plea slicing through the tension. "From now on, you'll do better at staying safe and not making rash decisions?"

"Matt—" My promise teetered on the brink of another lie.

"Can you?" His eyes were a challenge, a silent scream in the stillness of our home.

"Matt, I—"

"I can't keep doing this, Eva Rae." He cut me off, the finality in his words slamming into me with the force of a verdict.

The door shuddered in its frame as he left, the sound echoing like a shot in the emptiness he left behind.

Epilogue

The door's echo faded, and I turned to Angel. Her blue eyes watched me, wide and unblinking, a silent witness to the storm that had just passed through our living room. I knelt, my knees pressing into the carpet, and opened my arms. Without a word, she toddled into them, her small body a balm to the raw edges of my heart.

"Mommy missed you so much," I whispered into her red curls, inhaling the scent of baby shampoo and innocence. Angel squeezed me back, her tiny hands patting my back in a comforting rhythm that seemed beyond her years.

"Mommy wanna play with me?" Her voice was hopeful as she pulled away, looking up at me with a tentative smile.

"Let's play," I agreed, brushing away the dampness from my cheeks. I took her hand, her fingers warm and trusting in mine, and together, we walked to the corner of the room where a dollhouse and an array of stuffed animals awaited her imaginative command.

"Tea party," she announced, picking up a plastic teapot and handing it to me. Her freckles danced as she grinned, lost in the joy of the game. I played along, pouring invisible tea into tiny cups, watching her delight in the whimsy of our shared pretend world.

"More sugar, please," I said, playing my part with a goofy exaggerated accent that earned me a giggle. For a moment, the weight on my shoulders lifted, replaced by the lightness of her laughter.

"Mommy, you funny!" Angel declared, her blue eyes sparkling with mirth.

"Only for you, my little angel," I responded, allowing myself to be swept into the simplicity of the moment, cherishing the purity of her happiness. As we sipped our air-filled cups and chatted about her day, my resolve hardened. They would be my priority. This light, this love—I'd fight to keep it safe, always.

Through the laughter and clinks of plastic cups, I caught sight of Olivia lingering in the doorway, her slender figure uncertain. Christine came up behind her.

"Hey." My voice softened as I stood, abandoning the teacup. Angel's game momentarily paused as I moved toward them.

"Mom…." Olivia's word hung between us, cautious but hopeful.

"Christine. Olivia, I missed you guys." I opened my arms wide, an invitation they hesitated to accept before stepping into my embrace—one by one. Their bodies were tense at first but gradually melted into the warmth we'd missed for far too long.

"I'm sorry," I whispered, each apology tailored to the child I held. "For every night I wasn't here to tuck you in, for every game I missed, every school event… I'll make it right."

Christine's nod against my shoulder was subtle, her

rebellious streak softening just this once. Olivia, ever the composed one, offered a squeeze that spoke volumes.

"Don't be so hard on yourself, Mom," Olivia said.

Christine chimed in. "Yeah, you're out there making a difference. Not all moms can brag about that. I think that's pretty cool."

That made me smile. At least they seemed to understand and know who I was. It wasn't all lost.

We settled onto the couch, a tangled mass of limbs and hearts seeking connection. Their voices cascaded over one another, stories tumbling out about school projects and teenage dramas.

"Slow down; slow down!" I laughed, my heart swelling with every anecdote. "One at a time."

Olivia recounted her latest academic conquests with a pride that filled the room. Christine rolled her eyes affectionately at her sister's achievements but shared tales of her own adventures with a vibrancy that left us all grinning.

"Tell me everything," I urged, drinking in their words like a parched traveler. Their laughter, their squabbles, their dreams—I absorbed it all, recognizing the preciousness of these ordinary moments.

"I missed you, Mom," Olivia said quietly during a lull, her eyes reflecting wisdom beyond her years.

"Me too," Christine admitted, her goth facade slipping just enough to reveal the young girl beneath.

"Missed you more," I replied, the truth of it cutting deep. This was where I needed to be—where I should have been all along. My family, my heart, my home.

Matt suddenly edged into the room, a silent shadow detaching from the hallway's embrace. He hovered, a specter of mixed emotions, before sinking down beside me on the overstuffed couch. His presence was a gravitational pull, and I felt the shift in the room's atmosphere as the children's laughter dialed down to soft murmurs.

"Hey," I whispered, inching closer to him.

"Hey," he echoed, his voice a low rumble that seemed to reach inside and steady my racing thoughts.

Our eyes met, a silent conversation weaving between us. I saw the storm clouds there, the hurt, the love too—it was all written in the depths of his gaze. He didn't have to speak; I read the acceptance in the slight nod of his head, the way his hand found mine and held it with a gentle firmness.

I squeezed back, a silent promise passing through my touch.

Taking a deep breath, I turned my attention back to the kids, but my mind was racing. The chaos of the case, the close calls—they'd been a tempest I'd navigated by pure instinct. But here, now, it was the stillness that confronted me, the quiet realization of what truly mattered.

Family. Their faces, their futures.

I needed balance.

Epilogue

The whistle blew, piercing the afternoon air. I was on my feet, hands cupped around my mouth.

"Go, Alex!"

He darted across the field, a flash of blond hair and fierce determination. His lean frame wove between players with an agility that left me breathless, pride swelling in my chest like a tide.

"Mom, you're screaming louder than anyone," Christine teased, nudging me with her elbow.

"Can't help it," I shot back, grin wide as the ocean stretching beyond Cocoa Beach.

Alex's foot connected with the ball, sending it sailing toward the goal. The net billowed. Cheers erupted around us.

"Did you see that?" I said to Angel, who clapped her tiny hands, eyes alight with wonder.

"Your brother's a star," I said, sweeping her into my arms. Her laughter rang out, pure and infectious.

Matt's hand found mine, his grip warm and steady. We

watched Alex pump his fist in the air, teammates swarming him with high-fives and rough pats on the back.

"Kid's got your spirit," Matt murmured.

"Gets into trouble like me too," I quipped, but the familiar worry lines around Matt's eyes had softened.

"The good kind of trouble," he corrected, and I knew he wasn't just talking about soccer.

The game resumed… a blur of movement and energy. Olivia and Christine were on their feet now, joining in the chants and clapping rhythmically.

"Defense! Defense!" they chanted, voices melding with the crowd.

I scanned the field, watching Alex track the opposing team's striker. His focus was laser-sharp, every muscle coiled and ready. Like me on a case, except his battleground was green and open, his mission clear-cut.

"Nice block!" I yelled as Alex intercepted a pass, the ball ricocheting off his shin guard.

"Mom, really," Christine groaned, but her smile betrayed her amusement.

"Sorry, occupational hazard," I shrugged, knowing full well I'd be just as loud at the next play.

Time dwindled. Our lead held. When the final whistle signaled victory, the team erupted, a young, exuberant force flooding the field.

"Great game, Alex," I said, ruffling his sweaty hair as he jogged over, a grin splitting his face.

"Thanks, Mom. Did you see that goal?"

"Couldn't miss it," I said, pride lacing every word.

As we packed up our things, I caught sight of Matt watching Alex with a gentle gaze. It was a look that spoke volumes and said he understood the sacrifices, pain, and love that bound us all together.

"Ready to go celebrate?" I asked, slinging an arm around Matt's shoulder.

"Absolutely," he replied, and there was a lightness in his voice I hadn't heard in too long.

We walked off the field together… a family united, each step forward a commitment to what lay ahead. There were no guarantees in life or work, but there was this—a moment under the Florida sun, surrounded by laughter and cheers, where everything felt possible.

THE END

Afterword

Dear Reader,

Thank you for reading Dark Little Secrets (Eva Rae Thomas #16). I hope you enjoyed it.

The idea for this book came to me when I read a story about a woman who received a call that her son-in-law had been arrested for the murder of her daughter when the family thought it was just an accident. It sparked my interest, and I kept trying to put myself in her place, and that's when I spun my own story from it. If you want to, you can read more here:

https://www.nbcnews.com/news/us-news/scott-sills-susann-murder-husband-fertility-doctor-rcna150322

As always, I want to thank you for all your support. Don't forget to leave a review of this book if you can. It means the world to me.

Take care,

Afterword

Willow

About the Author

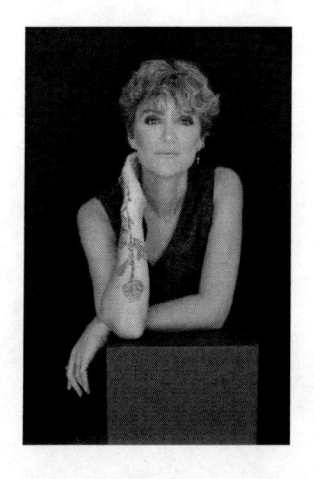

Willow Rose is a multi-million-copy best-selling Author and an Amazon ALL-star Author of more than 100 novels.

Several of her books have reached the top 10 of ALL books in the Amazon store in the US, UK, and Canada.

She has sold more than six million books that are translated into many languages.

Willow's books are fast-paced, nail-biting pageturners with twists you won't see coming.

That's why her fans call her The Queen of Plot Twists.

Willow lives on Florida's Space Coast. When she is not writing or reading, you will find her surfing and watching the dolphins play in the waves of the Atlantic Ocean.

Join Willow Rose's VIP Newsletter to get exclusive updates about New Releases, Giveaways, and FREE ebooks.

Just scan this QR code with your phone and click on the link:

Copyright Willow Rose 2024
Published by BUOY MEDIA LLC
All rights reserved.

No part of this book may be used or reproduced by any means, graphic, electronic, or mechanical, including photocopying, recording, taping or by any information storage retrieval system without the written permission of the author except in the case of brief quotations embodied in critical articles and reviews.

This is a work of fiction. Any resemblance of characters to actual persons, living or dead is purely coincidental. The Author holds exclusive rights to this work. Unauthorized duplication is prohibited.

Cover design by Juan Villar Padron,
https://www.juanjpadron.com

Special thanks to my editor Janell Parque
http://janellparque.blogspot.com/

Made in United States
Cleveland, OH
13 January 2025